# WITCH 6

TYLER SEHN

*To those who accept that pain is a sign of healing*

# PART I
# OF MATTERS MATERIAL

The harsh clang of a hammer rang out again and again.

An ancient blend of human intention and handheld skill.

A scent of hot steel mingled with the sweat of labour.

Mavrik hovered over his task, eyes unflinching as he brought the hammer down. He bent the rod around the anvil horn, shaping glowing steel into a form meant for an animal that had never set foot on this world. Next, he set the horseshoe atop the flat surface of solid black iron, the object quickly losing colour as the air swallowed its energy.

Such is the way of physical creation.

Mavrik replaced the hammer for tongs, gripping the horseshoe and plunging it into fresh water he had personally sanctified. Steam hissed, sealing the essence of the steel. He placed the dark crescent on the table and set to preparing himself to transform the object into a numanen. This would be his sixth idol, an impressive display of Anima, unseen for generations. Mavrik washed his face and tucked away the braids that had come loose, excited at the thought of success.

He might be a serviteur, but no other witch had the stones to attempt what he was about to. This accomplishment would make him undeniable within society; they'd have to accept him regardless of his past.

"Prepare your Self," he said, pointing to the horseshoe.

Mavrik retrieved his handpan drum and sat facing the newly crafted horseshoe. He played the handpan slowly at first, using thumb, palm, and finger-pad. His hands teased a sweet percussive rhythm out of this steel drum contoured in the shape of a tortoise shell. The tempo increased, filling the room with sound. Mavrik added his voice, chanting in kallikrates, a language known only to witches. His words of *the beautiful power* merged with the music, strengthening the vibration, creating presence.

He focused this vibration on the horseshoe, directing the energy to flow into the object. With a link secured, he shifted his attention to a specific incorporeal being—a force he had sensed growing in strength for some time, lurking on the periphery of his dreams, whispering at the edges of his waking mind. The being awakened.

A shadow fell across the space between instrument and implement. The shadow coalescing into a shifting, menacing entity made of smoke. Hostility, sharp and dynamic, pushed out of this being summoned against its will. The smoke took on a humanoid form, its hands clenching and unclenching as it fought against Mavrik's influence. Mavrik fully observed this spy from another plane, finding the aura to be unfamiliar, conveying a flavour he did not trust.

He sang, voice wavering high and low as his hands pounded against the handpan. He uttered words of binding, striving to secure the shadowy form to the horseshoe and keep it in this plane. The being tore at the strands of energy, its fingers slicing like blades. It growled vehemently, disrupting Mavrik's vibration. This sudden reversal of energy shocked Mavrik as he winced against the onslaught.

His strands of binding were ripped away by dark hands reaching for his chest. Mavrik placed every ounce of attention into resistance. This other sought to possess him, to claim his body as its own.

Wisps of smoke infiltrated the kallikrates, seeping into Mavrik and imparting a foreign will. Foul yet strangely familiar, Mavrik was simultaneously repulsed and intrigued. A pair of smoky, pitiless eyes glared in his mind's eye as the entity slipped past another line of defense. Mavrik, beaded with sweat, strained to resist, desperately trying to end the invocation. He shouted a word of closure, erecting an invisible barrier. His hands lifted from the drum as if it were scorching.

Otherworldly silence pervaded the room. The smoky form vanished. The horseshoe had cracked in half. Mavrik's head drooped in exhaustion.

* * *

Kalubon, the Black Lotus, was the ninth planet to be inhabited by humankind following the exodus of Old World. It was a terrain dominated by vast jungle, wild rivers, and creatures similar to those in stories stretching from humanity's distant past. A pristine jewel in the eyes of the settlers.

Initially.

The planet seemed to have an aversion to technology; a quirk in the magnetosphere. Ships dropped from the sky like so many tons of dead weight when they attempted to land, their systems malfunctioning. Standard practices of colonization proved ineffectual as the machinery refused to cooperate. The ease with which humans had grown accustomed to when conquering a new world was shown to be a flimsy veneer.

Most travellers beyond the atmosphere noted Kalubon as a trivial anecdote, then forgot about it altogether. Many people moved on, content to find easier routes. But some stayed.

A few intuited the independence afforded by this world. They dreamed of a society outside of the Alliance's grasp. And these colonists soon discovered they were not alone. Something arcane remained. Magic, like a rat on a transatlantic cruiser of Old World, had stowed away and survived the cold, dark space voyage. Gods hadn't fared so well. Deities, like higher technology, were shut out by Kalubon.

People survived, and thrived, adapting to the environment, fundamentally altered after two generations. They came to realize Anima, the spiritual essence in all things. Thoughts changed, language mutated, and kallikrates was born. Those with the greatest aptitude became known as witches, at once beloved and feared for their ability to cultivate and express the mysterious. Witches were the first group to occupy roles in centralized administration, but as eras transitioned their guidance was almost completely subsumed by the bureaucratic Leadership Council.

The Omolaras persisted, this greatest of witch lineages retaining public influence. Yet even this famed family had fallen into disrepute. A single member remained to keep the bloodline alive. A serviteur, a witch for hire. A man slandered behind his back when others were certain he was out of earshot, even as they surreptitiously requested his services. Mavrik Omolara, known in certain circles as Sixfold, in others as Jackal; despised as a Two Handed Hoarder, respected as the Blood of Oberon.

* * *

Mavrik bathed in the river, cleansing himself of the lingering effects from the failed invocation. Bits of malice stuck to his aura like hooked burrs to one's clothing when barging through the jungle undergrowth. He washed methodically, careful to carry handfuls of flowing water over every area of his body, culminating by submerging his head and the five numanen hanging around his neck. A witch was obligated to display their totems of power, make visible their occupation.

Back on the riverbank, warmed by the heat of the rising sun, he walked uphill toward a craggy cliff-face, seeking a particular cave. Barefoot as always, he followed a narrow path of stones set into the earth, matching the sun in stride as he moved above the canopy. A trio of ravens observed his approach, their black plumage shimmering. He passed through an invisible boundary, triggering the smart motion detection alarm. The birds scattered, squawking at being disturbed as they winged further up the hill.

Glittering eyes and ruffled feathers awaited him at the mouth of a cave lit by soft electric light from within. The birds clacked their beaks then disappeared; the familiars departing from this plane. Mavrik strode into the cave, desiring advice from his mentor.

Imamu, elderly, dark, merciless and as giving as Nature was seated on a circular rug. She gave him a momentary glance and snorted. "Still a measly Sixfold."

Only Threefold herself, although the connections were exceptionally strong.

"The entity hid its form. All I could see was smoke and shadow. I thought it to be a psychopomp like the others, but its behaviour was strange."

"What did you feel?"

Mavrik turned to the cave-mouth, peering into a world of warmth, of light. "Pain and hate."

She waved a hand in casual disgust. "Think no more of this damaged soul-guide. Not one to become a familiar."

He chewed on the truth of her assertion, finding it indigestible. "The pomp knew me. It has sought me out specifically."

Imamu's fierce eyes locked onto him, seeming to glow in the cave dimness. "Sinister intent, I suspect." She patted the rug. "Come, we shall learn."

Mavrik brought her ten candles, which she set around herself in a circle while speaking kallikrates. She cracked open a ripe pomegranate, its flesh and red seeds to be given as an offering. Her tattooed hands reached for the jade idol hanging from a cord around her neck—a numanen housing a familiar known as the Diviner. Imamu sang liltingly, the beautiful power opening doors between dimensions of existence.

The candles flared, flame stretching high and thin. Pomegranate redness blackened into char as the vitality was absorbed. Imamu's singing ceased; she opened green eyes with yellow pupils. Her hands released the numanen, upraised palms displaying swirling spirals.

"Diviner," said Mavrik. "Please use your vision to discover the cause of my recent affliction."

Diviner smiled, lips painted a frostbitten blue. "Clarity aids vision."

"What is the meaning of this psychopomp who watches from behind shadow, who grasps at me with smoke?"

The familiar brought her hands together in a sign of prayer. Her eyes were open, unblinking, able to see into time as a human views space.

"Your visitor grows impatient," said Diviner. "A great journey approaches." Her lips pursed in concentration. "A hunter." Her brows furrowed, heavy lines creasing her forehead. "Bound to you throughout the planes. Not a psychopomp. No, something else."

Diviner grimaced, struggling to maintain her vision. "It knows I look. It comes for me."

The familiar gasped, eyelids fluttering as Imamu's body fell backwards. Flames plunged into candle-wax, sending up wisps of smoke. Imamu twitched, coming back into her Self.

"Well?" she asked, rubbing knuckles into her eyes.

Mavrik meditated on the bizarre reading. Imamu sat upright, cracking her neck from side to side.

"Rude for a student to withhold from their teacher," she said. "If you were a patron I wouldn't ask."

Mavrik felt a low rumble in his bones, like a premonition of an earthquake. "Change has come. An unknown transformation."

The rumble intensified: why did it feel like the transformation had already occurred?

"Change is the only constant," she said.

"This is different. It feels unnatural."

"Lately, I have noticed fluctuations of Anima," Imamu said hesitantly.

Mavrik's world was violently shaking now, though he did well to conceal his terror.

"I will meditate on this," said his teacher.

"Thank you." He moved for the exit, shading his gaze from hers, lest the perceptive witch recognize his imbalance.

Mavrik returned to the spot downriver where he'd parked his strider, deactivating the user lock and climbing into the seat. The electrochemical battery initiated and a mass of carbon fibre tentacles pressed out from the bottom, raising the spherical body off the ground. Acceleration and braking were controlled by foot pedals in the stirrups. One hand commanded direction by scrolling on a round trackpad linked to the seat, capable of swivelling the driver in three hundred and sixty degrees. He flicked forward and the tentacles crawl-walked across the uneven jungle floor.

He passed through terraced rice paddies, entire hillsides transformed into emerald towers. Agricultural architecture fed the many mouths of Siridea, Kalubon's largest community. Then the jungle fell away from this space carved out in the name of humanity.

Mavrik locked the strider on target for the heart of the city, where a monumental geodesic dome resided, from which all settlement had expanded. The Dome's interior was separated into distinct districts situated around a central core where Leadership convened. Mavrik's business had nothing to do with Leadership or the Dome, it being considered a social impropriety for his kind to show their faces there. A serviteur was useful but uncouth, something beneath the ethics of an average Siridean—until certain services were needed.

Some people openly stared as Mavrik passed by, while others pointedly ignored his presence. Such things mattered when status, measured in social tokens, were as important as currency.

Despite his best efforts, Mavrik's family history was better known than his personal accomplishments. Such was the curse of being the last in a long line of infamous witches. His considerable skill in kallikrates only added to the rumours.

In the shadow of the Dome he turned down a narrow street where his office was located. This venue had been chosen for its adjacency to high society; a consideration for those who did not want to be seen in more illegitimate areas further from the center. He parked the strider and entered a doorway beneath a sign reading, "6."

The room was small and well-lit, with many ferns and shrubs lining walls adorned with geometric symbols. No one was at the front desk. Mavrik growled and pushed into one of the back rooms; the door opening at the touch of his fingerprints.

"Welcome home!" shouted Rouey, seated on a couch with his feet resting on a sculpted table of blackwood.

"How can I get missions if you're not out front?"

"You won't be needing any for a good long time after the fat catch I just reeled in."

Mavrik hesitated, more cautious than intrigued. "What is the nature of the request?"

Rouey waggled his eyebrows and motioned for the witch to join him. Mavrik sighed and slid a chair nearer, a feeling of sinking dread in his gut to balance his friend's rising optimism. Rouey waited, a smile slowly spreading over his face. He nodded at an object on the table.

"A numanen given as down payment. A vessel of the finest quality, in my humble opinion."

Mavrik leaned closer, eyeing the magical object as though it might sprout legs and skitter away. His intuition whispered danger. His hands itched at the potential. Rouey, as he often did, spoke the thought for him.

"Should be strong enough to hold that new pomp."

Mavrik sat back. "Suppose I already got it?"

"You're a terrible liar."

Mavrik smirked. "I am the Two Handed Hoarder, after all."

Rouey tapped his nose. "I'd smell it. Got a sense for truth. When you become Sevenfold they'll have no choice but to elevate your social status."

Mavrik set his feet on the table as well. "What else did this arrogant would-be patron offer?"

"The impossible."

Rouey got up and poured two glasses of his homebrew,

handing one over to Mavrik. He drank deeply then sighed, drifting back to the couch.

"The patron guaranteed a seal from Leadership declaring you to be a sanctioned witch. Your dubious history erased."

Mavrik stared into the drink like it was a bottomless pit. "A clean slate."

Rouey raised his glass in a toast. "A new beginning."

Mavrik grinned, in spite of his concerns regarding the risk, and raised his glass. He tilted the cup back and downed half in one go. "Ahh!"

He'd been waiting for an opportunity like this for most of his life. Ever since his father died, a death that had come after utterly destroying the family name. Ivaylo had been as hated as Oberon was beloved, leaving an uncertain path for Mavrik.

"We're still young enough to make something of ourselves," said Rouey. "Only twenty-five, just entering our primes."

Mavrik swirled the liquid in the glass, rolling potential futures around. "What's the ask?"

"A dark deed. You're not going to like it." Rouey finished his drink. "An important man is on his deathbed, unconscious and unresponsive to all treatments. Apparently, there are questions only he can answer, so, when he croaks, we will be contacted and you will return the aspect of him capable of speaking."

"You mean turn him into a zombie."

"Yes, I believe that is the colloquial term. Spooky."

"It is the ultimate sacrilege. A witch found guilty faces banishment, or worse."

"I know the stories, but surely it isn't that bad?"

"The dead is forced to come back, then it is violently murdered; the body doubly desecrated. The zombie must be burned before it is consumed by bloodlust."

"No one would have to know."

"All is known within Anima."

Rouey refilled the glasses, but neither drank, each sitting in the silence of their own thoughts.

"There once was a man of Kalubon in the times of the Deterioration," said Rouey. "A Siridean of unparalleled ability. He did what needed to be done even though the mob shouted accusations of sacrilege. An entire world was saved because one man had the courage to trust himself."

"My grandfather's Pilgrimage is not the same as this situation."

Rouey frowned. "I know. But one day Kalubon will need you and you won't be able to answer the call because of the bullshit status afforded to a serviteur. The people will doubt your intentions."

"I have no greater purpose."

Rouey's head snapped up, his eyes blazing. "You're an Omolara."

"My father acted with a similar entitlement."

Rouey tapped his nose. "I have a sense about these things."

Mavrik shook his head, then raised his glass. "To truth, may it be found in one's actions."

"No reward without risk!"

"I won't risk a decision just yet. First, I must tell you about an extraordinary morning."

The friends talked and drank, legacies and consequences temporarily displaced by a mystery.

* * *

Mavrik walked the crooked streets of his neighbourhood, trying to make sense of the incident with Diviner. This newest pomp that wasn't a pomp. She'd called it a hunter. An incorporeal being capable of lashing out at Imamu's intrusion. Choice and awareness of that magnitude should only be possible if the spirit had possession of a living person in this plane. To have a possession in any other sphere just didn't make sense. Shouts of alarm from nearby sharpened his wandering mind.

He caught a snippet of a scream cut short. The harsh fizz of a weapon discharge hitting metal. The violence was taking place in a nearby building, in what appeared to be a factory of some sort. No sign of Law Enforcement. Mavrik's hands were moving swifter than his mind, reaching for the tools of his trade.

He ripped free a red bandana that was tied around his arm and secured it over his eyes. Nimble fingers opened a small container to retrieve a pinch of gunpowder, which he snorted into both nostrils. A chant in kallikrates poured from his lips, fluid and compelling. His right hand went to a numanen: an ancient shell casing, spent ammunition from a projectile firing gun. Mavrik called on the Ronin.

A form rose out of the shell: a man wearing a wide brimmed hat, his lean face covered in stubble, his eyes penetrating yet tired, as though they'd seen things they'd rather forget.

"Subdue the assailants in that building," said Mavrik. "Kill if necessary."

The Ronin grimaced, tucking his thumbs into a belt with a silver buckle. A pair of revolvers on each hip. A black long sleeved, collared shirt replaced Mavrik's chest as the Ronin materialized. His dusty brown cowboy hat obscuring Mavrik's braids. The hard heels of Ronin's boots clacked on the street as he entered the building.


*Same old shit*, thought the Ronin. Once a triggerman, always a hired gun. Body and spirit, apparently.

He sidled into the entryway, ears perked. Nothing. No guard. *Sloppy sons of—*

The gun was in his hand and the bullet fired before conscious thought. A man lay dead at the end of the hallway. One more nameless victim added his body count.

He stepped over the body, eyes searching; a predator on the prowl. A warrior from a time and place that the horse he rode likely couldn't imagine.

Shots fired, crackling balls of electricity. The Ronin slid on by and returned fire, his otherworldly ammunition punching straight through walls. He found two more bodies with the life leaking out of them; blood pooling on the tiled floor. He paused, momentarily ensnared by the vibrancy of the colour, sensing the energy of life in it, the power of transformation in death. Life, something he couldn't have; death, all he could give.

Three gunmen jumped him and let loose. The Ronin blasted every remaining shot in the chambers, aiming for the incoming electricity. His bullets nullified the strange ammo, dispersing them into nothing. His hands were a blur as he reloaded and fired again. Three shots, three more dead.

He entered a large room full of mechanical engineering that he couldn't make heads or tails of. A scene in the center hit closer to home—a desperate man held his weapon against a frightened woman's head. The captor's teeth were bared, their eyes hard. She was panicked, ready to collapse.

"You are a mindless pawn," spat the man.

"No need for rudeness," said the Ronin. "Let her go and we'll settle this."

"Have you realized what they do here? What they are planning?"

The Ronin didn't like the crazed look taking over the other's features. It was the resolve of a person ready to die for a cause, ready to kill an innocent in the name of a grander mission.

"This is only the start," said the hostage-taker. "They will corrupt Kalubon itself. Enslave us all."

The Ronin saw the resolution made in the other, intuiting what was about to take place. He was quicker. The other dropped; the woman screaming as the body smacked against the floor. The Ronin put the revolver back in the holster. He took a long look around at a world he didn't understand. *Suppose I never knew my own world either. Some parts maybe, some parts too well.*

He tipped his hat to the woman, already beginning to lose physical form. Like an animated fog, he seeped into the shell and was gone.

Mavrik dropped to his knees, removing the bandana with trembling fingers. His vision was hazy, requiring a few moments to take in his surroundings.

"Are you hurt?" he asked the staring woman. "What happened?"

Her eyes rolled back and she fainted, landing unceremoniously beside her former captor. Hurried footsteps came from the hall, accompanied by the curt shouting of Law Enforcement.

"The situation is already taken care of," said Mavrik, rising.

"On the ground! Arms spread! Now!"

Mavrik grudgingly complied; a heavy boot crunching between his shoulders.

"Jackal," said the officer. "Why is it that you always seem to turn up when there's blood?"

"Things would be a lot worse if I hadn't intervened."

Boot treads dug into his back, pressing him into the floor.

"Damn vigilante. You aren't granted authority by Leadership. *We* are."

"I saved that woman. Stopped these hijackers from completing their mission."

"So you say." The officer tsk-tsked. "Going to take a miracle to clear your name after this one. Might be what finally brings you down." He laughed harshly. "Although, there isn't much further down to go, is there?"

Mavrik struggled wildly, frustration boiling over; his thin frame lacking the physicality to overthrow the other's oppression. A tase-jolt rocked his nervous system, causing him to spasm until his mind blanked.

* * *

Five hours in solitary confinement. No food, water, or bathroom privileges. Mavrik waited; he'd been through this before.

They must have spoken with the survivor by now and realized that he wasn't at fault. Still, they'd make the most of this opportunity and exact their anger. Hypocrites. Law Enforcement had solicited his services on several occasions when in a bind, through covert channels, of course. Despite his support, they refused to trust him, because a serviteur was a law unto itself.

A sanctioned witch had a code to follow, a serviteur followed the rules that were useful. Serviteurs occupied a grey-area leftover from the time when witches directed events, a remnant allowed to remain due to tradition and the occasional need to work outside of the law.

The door slid open and a man entered, obviously not an officer. He seemed to be around the same age as Mavrik, was slim, well dressed, and carried an air of unwavering authority.

"I am Director Ikenna. A member of Leadership Council," he said, claiming the second chair. "That facility you shot up falls under my jurisdiction of Technological Progress."

"The facility I saved from falling into the hands of insurgents."

"What do you know of this rebel group?"

"Nothing. I make this deduction from what little I've gleaned from my familiar who was present at the scene."

"You can communicate with it?"

Mavrik pointed at words carved into the table: *mutiny, zealots, sloppy*.

"I've had time to get creative," said Mavrik, bluntly indicating his boredom.

"They said you were different." Ikenna's face didn't change but his level of observation shifted. His eyes were like a set of tiny periscopes, focusing and refocusing. "The female survivor mentioned that your psychopomp was quite unusual. She called it, The Lonely Killer."

"Close enough." Mavrik shifted in his chair. "Are we finished? If you've spoken to her then you know my role in the event."

"Do I? You sent a known killer into a private facility for no apparent reason. Why not contact Law Enforcement? Why take the risk? What did you hope to gain?"

"Some of us actually care about the people who live here. Their lives are more than tools to further one's own career."

"Strong words from a serviteur." Ikenna rapped his fingers on the table. "You sought to enhance your name by playing the hero. Courageous, if it wasn't so pathetic."

"I've been judged my whole life for things I'm not responsible for."

Ikenna's composure slipped, his lip twitching into a snarl. "Because you're an Omolara. Your father, Ivaylo, attempted to fracture Leadership, manipulating the goodwill engendered by his father. There were rumours that Ivaylo had a following. Perhaps these rebels are remnants of his cult. Members that you silenced to hide your own involvement."

"My involvement in what?" Mavrik leaned closer, inwardly pleased to see Ikenna press hard into the backrest. "Your facility, what sort of *technological progress* is done there?"

Ikenna's bureaucratic stoicism returned. "That's classified information."

"Seems like you're hiding more than I am."

"You have your secrets, of that I'm sure. Your family is full of them." He tapped his fingers along the table edge. "There's one I've always wondered about; how is that your grandfather and his twin brother both started the Pilgrimage, but only Oberon returned?"

"I don't know. I wasn't there."

"It is the curse of those in the present to inherit the past. You'd think we all receive the same gifts, but sadly that isn't the case. From this unequal starting place, we all struggle to control the future."

"Control is for Leadership. A witch supports Anima, the spiritual essence of all things."

"I wonder what the men you murdered would think of that?" Ikenna stood up. "I hope you've learned your lesson."

"Likewise."

The Director departed, leaving Mavrik in solitary confinement once again. Two hours later he was released; greeted by a worried Rouey.

"I'm sick of this," Mavrik hissed as soon as they were back on the street. "I'll take the deal. It's time to leave the serviteur life behind."

* * *

"Tell me again," said Rouey.

Mavrik rolled his eyes. "We've been over this."

Rouey reached out and grabbed Mavrik's chin, turning the witch's attention back to him. "Banishment. Or worse."

Mavrik swatted away the hand. "You vetted the patron. I trust your judgement."

The patron was the wife of a senior Leadership Council member, who was probably after the private vault combination.

"Yes, her story checks out, but let's make sure that you know your part in it."

"Fine." Mavrik raised a fist to count off the steps on his fingers. "At midnight I take the unmarked transport that you have arranged. I arrive at the residence: 222 Skyline Heights in the Dome. I take the secondary walkway to the rear entrance. I knock three times. I make a zombie of a dead man." He showed a hand of five fingers.

"Come on, Hoarder, get them both up."

"I leave through the rear entrance, where you will be waiting with my strider. We exit the Dome by a more creative route. We return here, barricade the doors, and wait for Leadership's sanction, which will arrive at noon tomorrow."

Rouey exhaled heavily. "If you get into trouble?"

"I activate the transponder by biting down on my fake tooth." Mavrik smiled. "And then?"

"I light up 222 and get you the hell out of there."

"It suddenly occurs to me that I won't require your service once I'm sanctioned."

"You wouldn't last a day without me."

Mavrik extended a hand and gripped Rouey by the forearm. "Thank you, my brother. You have set me free."

Rouey's grip was firm, but his face appeared troubled. "We'll know for sure by noon tomorrow."

They separated and went about making final preparations for the mission, Mavrik keeping his doubts silent, never having undertaken a ceremony of this seriousness.

He knocked three times and waited, a hooded figure in the quiet of Siridea's most luxurious neighbourhood. Mavrik wore a jacket with a special hood designed to obscure his face from cameras. The door swung inward and he crossed the threshold, the action carrying a palpable sense of fate.

"You can take that off," said the male servant, pointing to the hood. "Internal surveillance has been temporarily disabled, for obvious reasons."

"I'll leave it on."

The servant looked to press the issue, then shrugged and led Mavrik deeper into the mansion. Signs of wealth were etched into the smallest details of every facet, triggering childhood memories of playing in his grandfather's home. His last memory from that time was a heated argument between his father and grandfather that had forever closed the doors on that chapter of Mavrik's life. He could still feel the cold anger radiating from Ivaylo as he'd stormed out.

No strong emotions tonight in this house, only the weighty stillness of too many unused rooms. The servant gestured to the open doorway of the master bedroom where the patron waited.

"I'd like to see your face, witch," said a dignified woman, her hands of many rings clasped together.

"No need, it won't be my face that does what you've asked."

She stiffened slightly, eyes flicking to her husband's corpse. "Will he know it was me when he wakes?"

"He will not be human."

She swallowed hard, then nodded. "It must be done. Begin."

From an inner pocket, Mavrik withdrew a wooden mask that had been polished to a bronze sheen. The eyes were thin slits and the mouth open. A family heirloom and tool of the craft. He placed the mask over his face and removed the hood.

He sang in kallikrates and began dancing; specific movements corresponding to certain phrases. The speed of his dance increased to match the cadence of his words. Power and precision fused with intention. The ceremony built to a frenetic pace, creating a sphere of energetic confluence around the witch. Mavrik reached for the numanen—the tip of a human finger bone. A sudden, ominous hush clamped down on the bedroom.

Cackling laughter banished the silence, at once joyous and malevolent.

"Domagoj," said Mavrik, calling to the Sleeper. "A resurrection dance is requested for the man on the bed before you."

More laughter. Skeletal features flickered on Mavrik's mask. A tall, black hat with a peacock feather pinned to its side appeared atop his head. His jacket replaced by a long black coat adorned by brass buttons.

Mavrik turned to his patron. "Make no deals with him."

The mask was completely substituted for a skeleton's grin. Bony fingers protruded from dark sleeves. Domagoj removed his hat in a sweeping bow to the woman.

"Well met, madam."

She stuttered out something unintelligible.

"Alcohol, if you please. Some tobacco as well."

She peered around the room, as though the requests might suddenly materialize.

Domagoj tapped a foot impatiently. "Do hurry. Our time is short and my manners are wearing thin."

She called for the servant and gave the order.

Domagoj swirled a voluminous glass of red wine, avidly puffing on a cigar. He drank and smoked, walking leisurely circles around the room. The wife watched from the corner, hesitant to interrupt.

"Ah, the world of the living," he said. "Such flavour and fire!"

"Uh, yes."

"What's this?"

Domagoj fished around in his mouth, tugging out a tooth. He held it aloft, turning it to be seen from multiple sides.

"This isn't mine." He tossed it over his shoulder and sipped the wine, swishing it around in the newly made empty space.

"Shouldn't you…" she bit down on the rest of the question.

"Your husband's return won't be pleasant." He fixed her with a dangerous smile. "Not pleasant at all."

He drained the wine and snuffed out the cigar on his tongue. He whirled on the woman, pointing an accusatory finger and hurling the glass at her feet. She screamed, covering her face from glass shards.

"You commit a terrible act against the life of your beloved! Know that what comes next is upon your spirit. May what you seek be worth the price."

He crossed the floor in two quick strides to lean overtop the dead man. He spit into a palm and used a finger to stir the purplish-grey fluid into a paste, drawing lines and symbols on the man's face, nodding in assessment of his handiwork. From a sleeve he procured a long needle, which he held above like a maestro guiding an orchestra.

With absolute thoroughness, he moved the needle over the body. At certain spots the needlepoint vibrated and Domagoj muttered words to himself as he focused the energy. Then he plunged the needle into flesh to reanimate the body. Once satisfied, he put the needle away and removed his hat, reaching into its depths. He withdrew a spider, slick and foul as fresh oil.

The woman gasped, hand to mouth. The Sleeper cast withering scorn in her direction, then placed the creature on her husband's forehead. The spider dashed for the mouth, prying at the lips with several legs, and finally disappearing inside.

"Have your question ready," said Domagoj, not bothering to look at her.

The man shook, limbs flailing, neck jerking from side to side. A wail of utter torment tore loose. Bloodshot eyes snapped open. He sat up, sniffing like an animal.

"Ask," said Domagoj, in a hoarse whisper.

The wife mustered her courage, even taking a step closer. "What is the energy source needed to activate the Harvester?"

The zombie's teeth clacked and gnashed. Purple veins streaked its forehead. "Access the portal in the constellation of the Shepherd King. Target Errai, the bright star at the peak of the crown."

"How is the portal accessed?"

Ragged laughter dripped from a head tilted back at a crazy angle. She shuddered, but pressed nearer.

"How is the portal accessed?"

The zombie snapped its head into position, its eyes ravenous. "Come here, I'll whisper it to you."

She moved forward a half-step. The zombie lunged, curved fingers ready to latch on.

Domagoj swept in-between, swinging a grey sickle. The zombie's head tumbled to the floor, but its hands kept reaching. Domagoj brought down the curved blade, lopping off both hands at the wrist. Arms thrashed about as the zombie tried to free itself from the tangle of blankets on the bed.

"You'll want to burn the body," said Domagoj. "Every piece."

She watched the spectacle on the bed.

"I could dispatch of it for you," he said, "if we are able to reach an agreement."

Her blank eyes turned to him.

"A simple deal and your problem will be solved."

The zombie, out from under the blankets, leapt off the bed to stagger around the room. The wife shrieked and fled.

Domagoj tucked his weapon under an arm and removed his hat to repeat the sweeping bow. "Farewell, madam."

His form shifted, vaporizing as it descended into the numanen.


Mavrik's sight was limited to the slits in the mask. His tongue made coarse from wine residue and ash. There came a crash at the other end of the room as well as a garbled shouting. He removed the mask and tucked it away. The room was a nightmare.

A headless, handless body was repeatedly attacking a padded chair. Two hands flopped on the floorboards like fish on a riverbank. A human head lay on its side, eyes mad and roving, mouth snarling and biting at nothing. His patron had gone.

"Being a witch isn't enough. It seems I'm the custodian as well."

Mavrik took a sheet from the bed, twisting it into a thick cord. He crept around the zombie's body as the brute disentangled itself. Mavrik righted the chair and waited. As the zombie lunged to attack its four-legged adversary, the corded sheet looped around, snugging the body tight against the chair. Mavrik pulled hard, tying off the sheet ends. The zombie raged, crashing down with the chair, but the knot held. Mavrik closed the door and made for the exit.

The servant approached, outfitted with gloves, body armour, and a riot helmet. A firearm was slung on a strap over his shoulder. He carried a disposal bag and a hempen rope. Mavrik nodded and let the other pass, receiving a feeling of the servant's inexperience despite his preparation.

"Destroy every piece with fire," said Mavrik. "Good luck."

Mavrik thankfully stepped into recycled Dome air. The stars shone from above, the rounded ceiling made transparent at night. A glittering sprawl of electric light came from below, radiating outward in circles from the central pillar of Leadership. This privileged suburb resided on the highest platform in the living area, providing an unparalleled vantage. It could be easy for a person living here to think that the scene below included all that Siridea had to offer. His strider skidded into view. Mavrik hopped on the seat behind Rouey and the tentacles carried them away from Skyline Heights.

"You're not wearing your hood," Rouey admonished.

"Things got a little messy."

"Then why didn't you activate the transponder?"

"I handled it."

Mavrik's tongue felt the hole where his fake tooth had been. When had he lost that? Where? Best not to mention anything to Rouey, it would only increase his worries.

Rouey veered off the street, climbing over a residential wall, across a small lawn, and over another wall. The strider sped along a service road, then down some half-finished scaffolding in a construction site. In a few moments they had descended an entire stratum of society. Rouey turned sharply, crawling into a near vertical drainage channel and onto a lower level. The strider scrambled out of the crevice and accelerated down a main street. They merged with the traffic steadily flowing in and out of the Dome.

Mavrik tapped Rouey's shoulder at the entrance to their street. "Keep going."

Rouey hesitated for a breath before moving on. Mavrik's tongue kept prodding the empty space in his mouth; the sensation unsettling him, hinting at an unknown danger.

They drove into the night, leaving the city behind, passing through mountainous shadows cast by the terraced paddies and entering jungle darkness. The strider finally stopped, sending up a screech of ravens.

* * *

Mavrik is leaving home and never returning. He is dreaming, this he knows, because his mother puts a finger to her lips. *Quiet. Careful.* She winks. *Be brave.*

They are outside now. Running. They have to get away before his father comes looking. And Ivaylo will come.

She tells him to hide. There is an argument; anger exploding into conflict. Ivaylo's roar is matched by his mother's scream. Then silence.

He comes out of hiding, already knowing that he will be alone from now on. He can physically feel the loss of them. An absence with a terrible mass.

He's back at home; instantaneously transported. Small hands take the wooden mask and put it in a bag with other items. Ivaylo has trained him diligently in kallikrates, his mother has taught him how to think, how to survive. He steps out of the front door, leaving it open behind him.

* * *

Rouey slept on a cot in the corner, his back to the cave entrance. Mavrik, woken by fitful dreams, sat and watched the delicate touch of sunrise glide into stone nooks. Each dark space, no matter how small, eventually filling with gold. Three ravens hurtled into the cave, coming to rest before Imamu.

"You were not followed," she said. The familiar departing as streaks of night disappearing into the dawn.

"How about sending them to my office and having them sniff around there?"

"If only I were able." She frowned, stern and compassionate. "You are that concerned?"

Mavrik shook his head, eyes downcast. "Something doesn't feel right."

Imamu snorted. "There are consequences when a witch casts a resurrection dance."

"Maybe I'm overthinking it. For all I know, my sanction is being prepared right now."

"You speak from fear and from hope; which is true?"

Mavrik changed the topic. "What of your deliberations? Have you discovered the cause of the Anima fluctuations?"

Imamu acted as if she hadn't heard him, instead preparing two mugs of herbal tea. She brought one to him and returned to her seat, the steam rising from between her hands.

"Clarity eludes me, despite an increasing number of disruptive pockets." She brought the mug to her mouth but did not drink. "I sent my ravens to a few trusted witches and they talk of ill patrons." She drank, closing her eyes against the vapor. "An illness of which these experienced witches are unacquainted with."

"The illness is the same for all the patrons?"

Imamu nodded. "A sort of inner wasting."

"Fatal?"

"Bit by bit." Imamu set down the mug, folding her hands in her lap. "I planned to ask you to call on the Satyr and investigate this further, but now, I am not so sure. You must not be distracted when handling one like him."

Chikere, the Satyr, was as powerful as he was unpredictable. He detested being controlled. Yet his correspondence with Nature was incomparable.

Mavrik sipped at the tea, mentally weighing the risk. He owed much to Imamu, this kind teacher who had taken in a wild child.

"I will do this," he said. "I can remain balanced."

Mavrik retrieved a hand drum made from the skin of a goat. He dug around and found a beater, which was a double-headed stick. He went over to where Rouey was sleeping and banged the drum, steadily and loud. Rouey rolled over, complaining.

"Better prepare yourself for an appearance of the Wild-man," said Mavrik.

Rouey bolted upright. "You're serious? Why now? I haven't even taken a piss yet."

"Hurry up."

Rouey hustled outside; claiming a spot near Imamu when he returned.

Mavrik sat at the edge of the cave, gazing over the jungle canopy. He struck the drum, light and quick, his wrist twitching like it was boneless. The rhythm increased, becoming almost erratic. His words of kallikrates came with a great deal of emotion, sharing a haunting quality. With a final impact he slammed the beater into the skin with a flat hand. He set the drum down and took hold of the numanen —a small wooden flute.

Muscled flesh replaced Mavrik's clothing as the Satyr came forth. A thick beard emerging out of a clean-shaven face. Tight braids transitioned into curly brown locks. Completely nude, Chikere stood with arms raised, calling out triumphantly at the sight of the jungle.

Chikere breathed deeply, taking in all the layers of nature surrounding him. Embracing him! He felt joyous, his very Being bursting with life. Pleasure that could easily slide into mania.

Ecstasy.

"Chikere," said his invoker, "what is the cause of the recent Anima fluctuations?"

The command within the question centered him, forcing him to focus. He quested outward, sensing the wider energetic field for disparity. All was unity. This searching was useless. *Wait, what is that?*

It felt like digging. A foreign presence gouging into Anima, into everything. Into him.

This intrusion was an offense. "You are but a splinter!" He paced along the cave-mouth, attention locked on this distant intruder. "I shall pluck you out and snap you over my thigh!"

But the question had been *what*. He did not know. Something new. His focus waned, his thoughts returning to their usual track. A scent in the air, nearby; a female.

Chikere faced into the cave. "Come with me, woman. I will treat you to pleasures you dare not believe possible."

Fully erect, the Satyr strode into the cave. A man jumped up to block his path to the woman.

"You may join as well, fine sir. I do not judge."

"Easy now," said the man. "Everyone stay calm."

"Disrobe," said Chikere. "Shed your woven shackles."

Instead of complying, the man raised a hand in defense. "Stop!"

Chikere did not care for that word. He lashed out and gripped the man by the wrist, tossing him away as though the other weighed nothing.

"Woman—"

Now on her feet, she struck at him with a heavy stick, cracking him across the shoulder. He instantly felt the impact of the wards sunken into the wood.

"Be gone!" She whacked him again. "Be gone!" Whack. "Be gone!"

A final crunch to the stomach had him doubling over and turning misty. Chikere slowly dissipated, drifting into the numanen through the holes of the flute.

Mavrik staggered, holding himself in pain. Rouey walked slowly over, also groaning.

"I knew I shouldn't have asked," said Imamu, still hefting the club.

Mavrik rubbed his shoulder. "Anything useful before I lost control?"

"He called it a *splinter*," said Rouey. "Then he got horny."

"What happens if a splinter isn't removed?"

"Infection," said Imamu.

"Well," said Rouey, "I'm just glad I wasn't forcibly disrobed." His gaze traveled inward into memory. "Unlike last time."

Embarrassed, Mavrik instigated a return to the city. No Law Enforcement lying in wait for them. Neither did they find a sanction. Just a tooth placed on the front desk.

* * *

Rouey, furious about being cheated, had stormed out to check with his contacts regarding the status of the Skyline Heights patron. Mavrik was strangely calm, his thoughts circling on the puzzle this mission had become. Someone was playing a game with him.

A psychopomp with the capability of actualizing a resurrection dance was rare; a witch willing to take the risk was even rarer. Mavrik and Domagoj were on a short list to be entrusted with such a dangerous affair. The penalties associated with zombiefication for a non-witch were just as severe. Perhaps the sanction was never really feasible, but the return of his fake tooth implied a brash confidence. Someone considered their Self untouchable.

Then there was the down payment, the gifted numanen—a palm sized obsidian mirror. The object was perfectly polished, round, and the thickness of a finger. A witch of considerable skill had invested a great deal of time in its creation. Mavrik chose to begin his investigation here, rather than diving down rabbit holes of speculation.

He crushed herbs and roots with mortar and pestle, preparing a potion to access his familiar, Danya, also known as the Naga. She understood the subtleties of humankind that kept one alive, or hastened one's death.

Mavrik blessed a bowl of water, then dumped in the crushed plant matter. He drank deeply, trying to ignore the foul taste as streams of water dribbled down his chin.

Next came kallikrates; at times slow, other times harsh, but always in a whisper bordering on a hiss. He gripped the numanen—a metal cross with a snake coiled around it.

His hair descended, changing from black to an auburn bound by silver threads. Intricate bracelets appeared on his forearms. Dark, painted lines around the eyes. A flowing gown, immaculately white, lightly resting on her feminine form.

"Danya," said Mavrik, "track the numanen on the table back to its creator."

She traced her fingernails over the surface of the mirror, teasing out the dormant energy inside. Strands of power slowly lifted like snakes before a charmer. There was a sense of sameness between the strands, a spiritual fingerprint passed on by the creator. Danya swirled a single energy-line around a finger, then pressed her hands together. She sang, using a language that had died on Old World before the Exodus; her words travelling down the line.

The numanen resisted her intrusion, its interlaced structure was strong and unforgiving. Danya pushed harder, her eyes flashing fiercely. The deeper she went, the stronger the power of the numanen. In her fervor she crossed a threshold where the sacred object now had a grasp on her. This invisible tug of war carried on as both entities fought for dominance. There could be no partial victory here; one side would concede, and in doing so be forever altered.

Danya repeatedly advanced only to hastily retreat and re-attack from a different angle. Her voice filling with anger as the battle raged. A forked tongue flitted between her lips. She unleashed a torrent of energy, driving into the numanen in a wild rush. The connecting strand around her finger snapped. A vision appeared in her mind's eye: the creator's location.

Enraged, Danya bolted from the room, intent on tearing this person limb from limb. She stalked through the streets, focused only on the intuitive tug of the directional impulse. The world around her was of no consequence, only vengeance mattered.

Finally, the scene from her vision matched that of reality. Danya smiled mercilessly. She reached for the door, except her hand didn't move. Her feet wouldn't move either. The host was attempting to reclaim authority.

"I will not be denied," she spat.

"Your mission is concluded."

Her hands balled into fists. "This insult will not be forgotten. An offering is demanded the next time I am called upon."

Danya's form rapidly entered into the cross.


Mavrik gasped for air, choking on Danya's wrath. The Naga wanted blood. And she would get it if he ever wanted to access her again.

He was alone on a quiet street, which offered the privacy to collect himself. The four-story building had no windows and a single door. Mavrik tried the door; locked. Abandoned structures on either side. He noted the location, promising that he'd return.

On the walk back to his office Mavrik concentrated on his breathing, gradually easing out the stress placed on his body from Danya. She'd utilized a sizeable amount of Anima in proportion to what he was used to. Any more and she would have seized the reins completely. He was wearing himself too thin. First the incident with Chikere and now this.

He'd just settled into a chair with the last of the homebrew when his friend burst into the room. Rouey snatched the glass away and slammed it back.

"Our patron," he said, "the loving wife. She's dead."

"How?"

"Ruled a suicide."

"Why go through the trouble to create a zombie only to off yourself right after?"

Rouey dropped onto the couch. "Guilt? For what she'd done."

"Didn't seem to have any remorse when I saw her."

"Maybe she couldn't handle what she learned."

"Maybe the information is more valuable than she realized."

Rouey squinted. "What do you know?"

"I found where that was made," he said, pointing to the mirror.

"And?"

"Another layer to the mystery."

"Care to tell me?"

"I'll show you." He nodded at the storage closet. "We'll need the kit."

Rouey's eyebrows lifted at that.

"But first, I need to rest."

Mavrik hauled himself out of the chair, barely making the steps to his room, and collapsed into bed.

* * *

They scoped out the location for the next thirty-six hours, one stationed in front and the other at the rear. No one entered or exited. Yet, from inside came the periodic sounds of machinery at work. They assumed an underground access point, perhaps through an indoor market three doors over. Too many people to keep track of in order to identify suspects. Instead, from out of the kit, Rouey released a small drone to scan the building for cameras and a security system. The scan came back clean.

The kit was a remnant from their younger days when missions were scarce. It contained a selection of tools used for burglary. Rouey grabbed a depth finder and pressed it to the wall.

"Hmm, that's strange." He tried a second wall, then another, until testing all four. "Two feet thick of reinforced concrete." Rouey shook his head in disbelief. "This place is a fucking fortress."

Mavrik put the drill and probe camera back in the kit. They couldn't get through a barrier like that. The cutter might be able to get them inside, if given enough time, but they'd be going in blind.

"New plan," said Mavrik. "We track down the servant of 222 Skyline Heights. He was no ordinary hired help. I guarantee he has details about all the happenings at that residence."

The two men gazed at the Fortress in a new light, seriously doubting that it housed a witch.

* * *

Rouey watched from a corner booth in the pub, sipping a drink while he waited. Any minute now, a certain former servant should be entering this dive; a far cry from the luxury of 222. Some digging had unearthed the name, Marshall Caeso, and the cashing in of a few personal favours had eventually led to this location. Caeso had been keeping a low profile since the sudden deaths of his employers, but like a crab on the beach at low tide, he would periodically crawl out of hiding.

In the midday lull there was only Rouey, the barkeep, and one other seated at the bar, each wrapped in the meandering silence of untold stories gripped tighter than their hands around simple glasses. The door opened, allowing spears of light to momentarily pry into the stillness. Caeso chose a stool at the bar, motioning with his hand for service.

He drank deeply and without pleasure.

"Surely you can be in no hurry," said the man two seats over, "even though you drink like there is somewhere you must be." He laughed heartily. "This is a place to sit with memory and to forget."

Caeso sipped thoughtfully.

"Zidati," said the other, with a palm pressed to his chest. "A man who has seen this bar once if I've seen it a thousand times. And I know that it attracts dreams. Not the good kind, no, we should not be so lucky, but dreams squandered, frightening dreams that wake one up in the middle of the night."

Caeso stared into his glass, then finished the drink. Zidati, seamless as karmic consequence, ordered another for Caeso.

"An offering," he said. "May it endow you with an equanimity that I so rarely find."

Caeso hesitated, his suspicion obvious.

Zidati made an exaggerated look of disappointment. "Please, I am a lonely old man. Allow me what small honour I can afford."

Caeso's hand slid unconsciously towards the glass. Zidati's pout transformed into a beatific smile.

"To the memory of greatness to which we once aspired, and the reality that has conspired against us!"

Almost unwillingly, Caeso smiled and raised the glass to his lips. Inspired, Zidati continued with increased vigour, sharing stories and speaking swiftly, often asking questions only to answer them as if knowing what this new friend would say. Caeso seemed to enjoy the performance, chuckling at the jokes and nodding at Zidati's answers.

Rouey, unnoticed by Zidati and Caeso, observed the scene in detail. He stuffed plugs in both ears.

The barkeep was soon drawn into Zidati's stories, moving nearer and nearer, then laughing and nodding along as well. Zidati's hands accentuated points as his voice resonated—gradually shifting the vibration of the room.

Rouey, because he knew to be aware of this change, averted his gaze so as not to look directly at the energetic bald man in the suit.

Zidati, in a burst of laughter, spit droplets of beer across the bar, many of which landed on the face of the barkeep. "Go to sleep," said the storyteller. The barkeep slumped to the floor.

Caeso smacked his thigh, thinking this act to be part of a joke. Zidati, suddenly serious, dipped two fingers into his glass, reaching over to dab the liquid on Caeso's forehead. "Be still," he said, and Caeso complied.

Zidati cracked his knuckles, his humour evaporated. "You, my friend, are far from home. Your employer, the wife, who did she meet? To whom did she repeat the words of her wretched husband?"

Caeso's eyes darted in panic, unable to move. Zidati flicked a few drops at him. "Speak."

He tried to resist the request, his determination transitioning into terror as he was compelled. "Director Ikenna. He came to the residence as I was disposing of the body."

"Did Ikenna have her killed?"

"I don't know. I think so. Maybe." Caeso forced himself to blink. "I ran after burning the body. He, it, was laughing inside the flames. This memory haunts me."

"I could make you forget," said Zidati, a feral glint in his eye. "But I won't. All actions make us who we are, and what would a person be if they were ignorant of their darkest moment?" He held up a hand. "Don't answer that."

Zidati leaned closer, his teeth now sharp as fangs. "In the yawning chasm of your heart, what do you wish for?"

"A new life. To be able to start over."

"You are in luck! I know how this can be done."

Zidati jerked in his seat, his body acting as though it belonged to another. He scowled, fighting for control, gripping the bar with both hands and twisting his neck to lock eyes with Caeso. "Kill…your…Self…"

Rouey left his booth, rushing over.

Zidati released his grip. "Ikenna! The name you want is Ikenna! I have fulfilled my obligation."

Caeso withdrew a knife, raising it purposefully. Zidati's form softened into smoke. Rouey reached for Caeso; too late.

The servant's blade drew a scarlet line across his own throat as Zidati drifted into a numanen in the shape of a gold coin. Rouey slowly removed the earplugs, eyes vacant as Caeso slid off the stool.

A serviteur sat alone at the bar.

Mavrik jumped off the stool and hurled it away. "Damn it! Bastard!"

Rouey placed a hand on his shoulder. "Come on, we have to go."

Mavrik crouched beside the dead servant and made a sign of blessing. "I'm sorry."

Groans came from behind the bar as the kallikrates induced sleep began to lose effect.

* * *

In moments such as this, Mavrik went to the same person time and again. Some men hid their pain with drink or drugs or violence, and others in the embrace of a woman.

"Things must be worse than usual," said Roseline, "you've spoken fewer words than the number of times we've fucked."

He lay with his head on her thigh, eyes half-lidded, his mind drifting. The room was warm with the scent of them and his body felt like some distantly attached thing. He took her wrist, kissing the back of her hand. She laughed and pulled away.

"I know all of your tricks! You will speak now or you will leave."

He glanced at her, upside down. "My body is not enough for you?"

"When we were younger, perhaps, but even then I understood how cheaply one can give away their body while hiding truth. What do you hold tight inside that soul of yours?"

"I wish I knew," he muttered.

"Another trick. No false pity to be received here."

His thoughts turned somber and with them returned the needs of the physical—his skin clammy, his bladder full. Exiting the bathroom, he went straight for his clothes, but Roseline was too clever by half; her hand resting on a ball of clothing at her side as she sat in bed.

"Don't run," she said. "Not from me."

He sighed and sat on the mattress, facing away. "I feel like I'm coming undone. The familiars have their way with me and I'm left to put together ill-fitting pieces."

"A difficult realization for one as proud as you."

"Being in control has kept me alive."

"There is more to life than survival." She moved closer, stroking his shoulder. "A life is constructed through intention. What are you building towards?"

She removed her touch and he knew she was not alluding to them.

"Forgiveness or vengeance. I haven't decided yet."

A part of her had moved on a while ago, accepting that their relationship would never progress. Even now he felt her slipping away, his own Self distancing from her tenderness.

"I believe that you don't know what to believe in," said Roseline.

He turned to her and saw that she was smiling and for an

instant he was blinded by the radiance of that perfect smile. A witness to beauty. He looked away, had to.

"I don't deserve your kindness."

"Nobody does. Deserve kindness, that is." She wrapped her arms over his shoulders, her hair tangling with his. "Yet we keep on giving it away, this gift."

He smiled, despite his mood. "You should be a witch and not I."

"I'm too innocent. The world needs serviteurs to navigate the grey for the rest of us."

"Each season since Oberon's return there are fewer witches, and most of those who remain are figureheads with no real power." He placed his hand in hers and squeezed. "Anima is becoming distorted, changes at the fundamental level of existence."

"So now we get to the heart of your worry. It is not your responsibility to save the world. Take care of yourself, for once."

"Fate has set a different path for me."

She moved beside him, placing both hands on his chin and turning his face to hers, eye to eye. "How can a person who doesn't even know their own wants be privy to the will of fate? Heal your Self, then move on to the sorrows of the world."

"Your kindness will be the death of me."

She slapped him, playfully, but hard enough to sting. "My kindness is not endless. I say these things to you as a friend, as someone who has seen the person inside the serviteur. The time for hiding has ended."

Diviner's words-of-seeing inside Imamu's cave came to him, striking his breastbone like a hammer: *a great journey approaches.* Mavrik kissed Roseline's forehead, then placed the chain of numanen's around his neck.

* * *

Where to go?

Each direction is equally meaningless when one is lost. The world had turned into a maze from which there was no escape, yet Mavrik felt as though he didn't quite fit inside. Caught within this paradox he wandered as a prisoner to his thoughts and emotions.

His rambling brought him within the Dome; the brain stem of Siridea. Vehicles whizzed on busy roads and drones whirred overhead, but these distractions could not persuade his state of unfocused persistence. His feet, unerringly, and much to his surprise, took Mavrik to his childhood home.

A large house in a fine district—an area for those climbing the ranks or those on their way down from society's highest echelon. Situated at the end of a crescent, there was a single neighbour of this unfortunate residence. Trees and hedges were overgrown in the yard. The home itself had not reached a condition of disrepair requiring it be torn down, but no one wanted to live in Ivaylo Omolara's house, so it had remained empty these many years. Mavrik approached on stiff legs, his father's presence growing stronger with each step.

"Curse you, old man," he said, reaching for the door.

Locked.

He heard his father's snort of derision, forcing him to be resilient. His mother's comforting words afterwards. Mavrik flipped open the lockpad and pressed a thumb to the screen. There came a solid click of release and the door opened to his touch. *Yes,* he thought, *this house has memory.* He stepped past the threshold, leaving the door open behind him.

Cobwebs laced the corners and a fine layer of dust coated the surfaces. Outside light tentatively stole through half-shuttered windows. He stepped softly, unconsciously preserving the silence, lest something be awakened.

He felt drawn to his old room, following a call from the secret space within. A place to hide if needed. A gift from his mother.

Mavrik's deft fingers slid the floor tiles beneath his desk, revealing a comfortable compartment. Packaged snacks and a container of water rested on a shelf. On the lower level, a small pillow and rumpled blanket lay amongst scattered toys and a digi-reader. His attention narrowed on an object carefully placed amid these forgotten remnants: a small, rectangular card with handwritten lettering.

His heart leapt at the possibility of a final message from his mother, then plunged at the thought of Ivaylo having discovered this secret. Mavrik, mouth gone dry, plucked up the card.

*I know you don't want to be found. The pain you must be enduring is truly terrible.*
*Remember that you are not alone. If you do return, please seek me out.*
*There is more to kallikrates than you have been taught. There are levels of Anima that most believe impossible. I can show you, if you wish.*
*-Oberon*

Mavrik's legs gave out. He stared at the card as if it were a rare bird that could fly away at any moment. Shock temporarily blanked his mind, quickly giving way to anger. Where was his grandfather's help on that fateful day? Surely the great witch knew what his son was capable of. Why not make every effort to find a ten-year-old boy whose parents had killed each other? Mavrik crushed the card in his hand, but couldn't let it go. His anger softened into sadness, melting into fantasies of what might have been.

But Oberon had died a year after Mavrik had left this house forever. Even that fantasy had an expiration date.

Mavrik sniffed back the tears that would not fall and left his home for the second time while bearing an intention of never returning.

A boy of eight or so watched him from the end of the walkway. He stared, curious and frightened, deciding whether to run. Bravery, and a childlike need to know, won out.

"Are you a ghost?" asked the boy. "My father says that house is haunted."

"Something worse. I'm a survivor."

Mavrik started to leave, the numanens bouncing against his chest.

"You are a witch," said the boy. "My father says the time for witches is ending."

Mavrik stopped. "Who is your father?"

The boy coughed, hacking violently as he ran off.

Mavrik raised his head, vision casting to the distance, a level higher to his grandfather's former residence. If the old sneak had found Mavrik's hidey-hole, then maybe he'd stashed something there as well. Intrigue gave way to despair. Mavrik started for his office. He needed to rest.

Why did it feel like he'd never genuinely rested in his life?

* * *

The room was shaking, the city heaving, the world groaning with friction. An intense surge dumped Mavrik out of bed. He woke with a start, covering his head as items toppled and crashed. The earthquake's force overwhelmed his senses, rendering time meaningless. Then, without proclamation, the shaking subsided, leaving behind a false normalcy.

Rouey burst into the room with a streamer in hand. "Reports are calling it the most powerful quake in Kalubon's history." He sat beside Mavrik on the floor, eyes scanning information. "Lots of collapsed buildings. Mostly outside of the Dome. People are dead or trapped in the rubble."

Mavrik winced at the pain in his hip. "Let's go."

Rouey glanced up from the streamer in concern.

"No familiars," said Mavrik. "Only my own strength."

They stepped out of the disarray of the office and into chaos: people shouting and screaming, huge chunks of debris littering the street, massive holes in familiar structures. Disoriented, they walked, taking in the scene, slowly comprehending the effects wrought by sudden change. They passed the factory where the Ronin had confronted the rebels—now a heap of thick slabs and sharp edges.

"I hope no one was in there," said Rouey.

A security team arrived, sirens blaring, lights flashing. They set about constructing a barrier around the destroyed building.

"Their doom is sealed now," said Mavrik. "Ikenna is burying his secrets."

Ahead, people were congregating around a housing complex, the urgency in their cries pulling Mavrik and Rouey over. They dug with bare hands, straining against the weight, struggling against the time that those below did not have. Finally, machinery arrived, able to sift easily through the heavy pieces.

Human hands pulled bodies out of the wreckage, some still breathing with only minor injuries. Many were mangled beyond recognition. Physically exhausted and spiritually horrified, Rouey and Mavrik finished this grisly work.

A group chatter began as the last of the debris was excavated, a whisper of blame. Hard faces brimming with emotion. A group giving voice to the despair.

"This is Leadership's fault," said one. "A consequence for using unsafe tech."

"A corruption of Anima," said another.

"They harvest energy and put the cost on all of us."

Heated murmuring spread throughout the group, crackling with frustration and anger. The loudest voices swiftly departing at the appearance of Law Enforcement.

"The death rate is the highest in this area," said Rouey, checking the incoming stats on his streamer. "Medics won't be able to keep up."

Mavrik surveyed the intermingling of officers, excavation crews, medics, and civilians all trying to make sense of the devastation. "I have to do more," he said.

Rouey nodded. "I'll help."

They returned to the office and Mavrik prepared to access Danya, the Naga. He cut off a braid of his hair and placed it into a chalice. With the tip of a knife he pricked a finger, dripping three drops of blood onto the braid.

"That's all you get," he mumbled.

In a separate container he made the potion. Gripping the numanen, he called out in kallikrates.

Danya's form came shrieking into existence. "So soon! I have not forgotten, even if you have." She spotted the chalice and sneered. "A pitiful offering."

Rouey entered, wearing a blue and white robe of healing.

"What has happened?" she asked.

"Carnage," said Rouey. "Indiscriminate and widespread. Your aid is needed."

Danya's features softened and she picked up the chalice; the contents transforming into green flame. She drank in full, appearing calmed.

"Come," said Rouey.

He wore a backpack filled with supplies she might need, as they were sure to encounter a gruesome variety of injuries.


Dull, unseeing eyes fell on Rouey's symbolic robe. Gazes flicked to the woman in white, her gown unblemished by dust or blood.

"Lady Danya offers what blessings she can," said Rouey. "No fee or obligation. No patrons. Today there are only those in need and those who wish to help."

Those who were able came forward and she went to those who were unable. Danya sang softly in her mysterious language, hands raised over each person as she examined their health. She set bones in their proper place, mending with the weave of her words. Rouey, when instructed, passed over herbs for internal bleeding and ointments to seal cuts and punctures. For some, all she could do was place a black leaf upon their tongue to take away the pain.

She entered a trance-state, relentlessly seeing patient after patient. Rouey's supplies dwindled, the bag emptying as a red sun descended.

"Incompetent!" she snapped, momentarily between patients. "I will do this myself."

Rouey noted the reptilian tint to her eyes, the thinning of her tongue.

"That's enough," he said. "Our mission here is ended."

She snapped at him, hissing and brandishing long fingernails. Several would-be patients flinched, moving away as quickly as they were able. A child wailed, frightened by what it had glimpsed in her changing form.

"You see?" he said, calmly.

"But I can save them," she said. "I *will* save them."

Danya, her face now distinctly reptilian, advanced on the terrified crowd.

"Look," said Rouey, extending a handful of her auburn hair. The ground at her feet covered in clumps.

Danya stomped her heel. The hint of a tail swishing under her dress.

"Remain in control," said Rouey.

Mavrik's face flashed inside that of the Naga in a brief battle of awareness before her form began to drift into vapour. Rouey stepped up to catch Mavrik, the serviteur's body limp, his energy drained.

"Not enough," he said.

"It will have to be," said Rouey.

Fear lanced into Mavrik's heart. "Call Roseline."

Rouey tapped her contact and after a brief delay her head appeared as a hologram projected by the streamer.

"You're alive," she said, relieved. "You both look awful. Where are you?"

Rouey displayed the scene, making her gasp.

"You're all right," said Mavrik. "Everything will be…"

A bone-deep exhaustion swept over him and he dropped into a void of dreamless sleep. Rouey called for a medic.

* * *

He walks in a land that he has never been to before. A place that feels like an illusion; realer than a memory yet immaterial. It's hot and dry and lonely. Beige scrubland extends into rolling hills, surreal when compared to the jungle he grew up in. On his left, a molten sun is draped by purple clouds and on his right he is watched by a huge, silver moon. Ahead is a three-story building made of wood.

Mavrik pushes through a set of swinging doors, entering a large space dominated by the scent of alcohol, tobacco smoke, and tanned leather. A solitary figure sits at a table, mildly surprised by Mavrik's entrance.

"Howdy," said the Ronin. The gunfighter stretched a leg beneath the table to push a chair out for his guest. "Have a sit. The drinks are on me."

The witch obliged, openly observing the rustic environment. "Am I inside the numanen?"

The Ronin shrugged. "Who can say? Don't get many visitors. I reckon you might be the first. Hard to keep track of comings and goings, what with time being absent in this place."

A shot glass of whiskey slid over to Mavrik.

"It's good stuff," said the Ronin. "Good enough, anyway."

Mavrik looked to the drink, then to the cowboy, trying to make sense of things. "You are the Ronin."

"Don't quite know what that means." He slugged back his own shot glass. "Suppose it'll do for a handle, seeing as my own name has gone missing."

"How can we be speaking if my body is not under possession?"

A light flared in the eyes below the wide brim. "Now I recognize you. Tasunka, the horse I ride."

"Seems we both wear improvised names." Mavrik smiled, draining his own glass. "I'm Mavrik."

He frowned, his voice going silent when uttering his name.

The Ronin leaned forward, forearms on the table. "That is mighty interesting. I heard you say it, but at the same time I heard you not say it. Completely canceled out."

Footsteps sounded on the boardwalk outside and the saloon doors swung open. The Ronin's right hand went to his pistol.

"I don't like the looks of this one," he said.

Mavrik recognized the interloper immediately, even with

the smoke and shadow mostly gone. The Hunter. A face covered by absolute darkness, with twisting smoke where the eyes should be. It had a man's body draped in tattered clothing a shade of storm cloud-blue. Arms were tensed, fists clenched.

"Hey, stranger," said the Ronin. "Have a sit and be sociable, otherwise you're welcome to move on."

Mavrik opened his mouth to speak and the Hunter charged. Ronin's revolver let loose a flurry of shots, Mavrik ducked, and then the table exploded into jagged shards. Mavrik hit the floor; overhead came more shots and the Hunter's oppressive aura.

"Out the back, Tasunka!" The Ronin reloaded as the Hunter circled, preparing for another charge. "I'll hold him off."

Mavrik dashed for a door set beside the bar countertop. The Hunter roared; frenzied and murderous. Revolver blasts traced the Hunter's path around the interior. Mavrik slammed a shoulder into the door and fell into silence.

* * *

Wreckage can be cleared and injuries addressed, but the repercussions of a catastrophe leaves behind invisible scarring in the days and weeks following the event. A person loses their sense of safety as the community is altered at the dimension which supports human life. Routine and normality are shown to be facades. The power of change, after being witnessed in an eruption of chaos, simultaneously makes some people timid while emboldening others. Mavrik observed much of both in the aftermath of the earthquake.

Rouey helped him to the couch, fatigued from another round of Danya's healing.

"You have to take a break," said Rouey. "The medics are nearly caught up."

"Are they? Or am I being blocked out? When they see me they see Jackal, a person chasing the weak and wounded for his own benefit."

"I'm sure there are some who disapprove of how many social tokens your recent services have accumulated."

Health Services, supported by Law Enforcement, hardly let him treat any patients today. The animosity of these groups was becoming more pronounced as their tolerance thinned.

Mavrik slid down to lay on his back. "Did you notice how many sick there were?"

"I'm not blind."

"That cannot be caused by the quake. Imamu's warning is proving to be more than a hunch. This illness is becoming widespread, yet Health Services is guaranteeing that it isn't contagious."

"And the rumours are barely contained. This rebel group is almost out in the open."

"There's a taste of conflict in the air."

"We know from Ikenna's involvement at 222 Skyline Heights that Leadership is dirty. Those in power will use violence to keep their power. If there is a fight coming, one side seems to have more weapons than the other."

"What side are we on?"

"Our own side, because no one seems to be on ours."

"Yeah? A two-man army?"

"The Ronin tilts the scale. The Sleeper probably has a powerful arsenal too."

"Don't forget the Satyr. Maybe I just let him loose to rampage both sides, take everybody out."

"Point taken." Rouey rolled his eyes. "Fighting isn't the answer. Still feels like we have to do something."

"We will." Mavrik forced himself to sit up. "Grab the kit. We're going to steal some information."

A week of staking out his grandfather's former house and they'd pinpointed an ideal timeframe to break in. Mavrik could have guessed as much, judging by the district, but he wanted to be sure. In the late afternoon, the children left for activities and minutes later mom crept over to the neighbour's, entering through the back door. Two hours later she strolled home with a satisfied smirk, ready to greet the kids. Last of all came the father, returning home after a long workday. There appeared to be a single servant, and this elderly woman went to her main floor room during this time, only exiting when the wife returned from her dalliance.

Ready to spring the heist for an artefact of suspected existence, Rouey removed the most valuable object from the kit. He released a small metal sphere; some of the highest-grade tech that operated on Kalubon. The sphere zoomed away, hovering a few inches above the roof, resonating at a particular frequency to suspend the alarm system. They confidently set foot in the backyard, targeting a section of ornate climbing vines attached to a lattice on the wall.

Hand over hand they went up, Rouey with the cutter slung over his shoulder. He set to work on a specific location on the second floor, carving a circle large enough to slide through. From inside they reset the piece so it wouldn't be noticed from outside.

Mavrik had chosen this spot, recalling it to be a closet; adding an extra layer of stealth to their entry. The closet also happened to be near his favourite room, the place where he'd spent most of his time with Oberon—the planetarium. If the old witch had hidden a secret for his grandson, this is where it would be.

The closet door silently opened and they prowled down the hallway towards the planetarium, an enchanting room that had made young Mavrik feel like he was traveling amongst the stars. As a boy he could walk the connecting paths of constellations and visit distant worlds. Mavrik's pulse quickened as they approached the open double doors to this magnificent room.

Several steps inside and it was painfully clear that the planetarium was long gone. The space had been completely remodelled, converted into a playroom out of a child's dream. Toys and games of every conceivable style. Items and apparatuses that Mavrik couldn't hope to name. His optimism deflated. Rouey looked at him expectantly and all he could offer was a slow head shake of disbelief.

"Put your hands up," said an elderly woman. "Turn around nice and slow and maybe I won't blast you."

Rouey swore as they both obeyed the command. The servant levelled a firearm at them, her expression disconcertingly relaxed.

"Probably thought you had the drop on me," she said. "I've served this house longer than you've been alive and I haven't been fooled a day in my life."

Mavrik squinted and swore. "Trineh? Is that you?"

She hefted the gun, her composure rattled. "No tricks."

He carefully dropped his hood. "It's me, Mavrik Omolara."

"Disrespectful to wear the name of the deceased." She peered hard at him and by the firmness of her mouth he thought she would shoot out of principle.

"I'm alive, and will remain so if you don't pull that trigger. I used to play in this room as a boy. Grandfather spent hours teaching me about the stars."

"Sure," she said, wryly. "I remember little Mav. I brought

them snacks just as Oberon was firing up the machine. What was the first constellation displayed?"

Mavrik smiled. "Easy. It was Grandfather's favourite. The Shepherd King."

Trineh's lip twitched, and her weapon lowered a fraction.

"Your hair was red back then," he said, "and short."

The firearm descended to her side as a trembling hand went to her mouth. "Little Mav. I thought...after what happened..."

"I think he may have left something for me. A gift. My guess was that it would be here."

She waved a hand flippantly. "No, no, he entrusted that to me before he passed." Her eyes shot open. "I never imagined! But he always believed you were out there somewhere."

"Excuse me," said Rouey. "Can I put my arms down?"

"Oh yes, right this way."

Trineh led them downstairs to her private room. She punched a code into a safe and removed a square box the length and width of her hands.

"I never opened it," she said. "Not sure if I could have. Witches and their kallikrates and whatnot."

She passed it over; the word *Eldorado* in gold lettering on the lid.

Breathless, Mavrik accepted the treasure. "What does it mean?"

"He didn't say." She wagged a finger at him. "That man had a lot of secrets, but even he didn't have the gall to fake his own death."

"I never faked—"

"What's done is done. I'm happy that I could fulfill this final request."

Rouey scratched his head. "How did you know we were here? We used—"

"An interference sphere. Yes, I know. A shit model; horribly out of date."

"By the way," said Mavrik, "we cut a hole in the wall in the upper hall closet."

"I already called for repairs. It'll be fixed before dinner."

Mavrik and Rouey looked to each other, realizing how thoroughly outmatched there were.

She shooed them away. "Now you two best go before the lady of the house gets back from her romp."

They were suddenly back in the yard, bewildered and exhilarated. Rouey didn't bother recalling the sphere.

* * *

Mavrik glared at the box, willing it to open. The obstinate object refused to acquiesce. Trineh's notion had been correct; Oberon had taken special precautions in its sealing. Rouey's research on Eldorado provided snippets of information regarding a mythical city of gold on Old World. A place that no one had found because it never really existed. Frustrated and impatient, Mavrik hopped on the strider, stashing the box in a travel compartment.

He stopped outside of the city to wonder at the terraced rice paddies; a gargantuan jagged line running down an entire hillside like a scar left by the quake. The towering green was split in half and seemed ready to break away. He was struck by the callous indifference of Nature; that hill provided countless calories for the people of Siridea, yet its destruction meant nothing to Kalubon. *We need the planet more than it needs us.*

At the cave he found his teacher in a deep, meditative state: her eyes shut, her soul traveling inward. Mavrik watched her perfect stillness and waited for her return.

Imamu's eyes fluttered open as she came to her Self, her face slack, vision drifting.

"Welcome home," he said. "You went far."

Imamu rubbed her palms against her cheeks and eyelids. "Truth wasn't coming to me so I went searching."

"And?"

"And why are you here? You only visit when you need something."

He placed the box between them. "A gift from my grandfather that I cannot open."

"Omolaras," she muttered. "Do you know why Oberon went on Pilgrimage?"

"To halt the Deterioration. Everyone knows this."

"And what about the Deterioration needed halting?"

"Too many witches were shirking their duty. Inadequate training led to the use of black magic and the casting of curses."

"Kalubon was on the brink of civil war. Why you think I moved out here?" She reached for the box, then pulled back. "Some welcomed the Deterioration, claiming it would offer access to Anima for everyone. Oberon's brother was a champion of this cause. Rather than fight each other, they went on Pilgrimage together. Only your grandfather returned."

"And Anima became more difficult to access. The siphons of the corrupt and false were cut."

"The trust in our kind has never recovered."

"My father didn't help with that perception."

"What do you know of this?"

He sensed her guardedness. "What happened?"

"Some people came to me claiming to be followers of Ivaylo, calling themselves 'Children of the Wolf.' They spoke of him like he was a liberator."

Cold, dark rage swarmed Mavrik's mind, choking the words in his throat.

"This is why I search for answers," said Imamu. "I didn't want to tell you. But here you are."

"The rebels."

Imamu nodded. "The fight never ended, just went underground. They asked if I will side with them."

"And?"

"I kicked them out of my cave. Said, I'll find them if I want to join and not the other way around."

The legacy of his family had a life of its own, infecting others so it could pull him back under its influence. An insistent presence trying to shape what he would be become. Imamu placed a hand on his.

"I mention these things about your family for a reason. Trust your teacher." She pointed at the box. "Pilgrimages and rebellions may have been styled around the meaning of Eldorado. When we open it, you get to choose your role in this mess."

Mavrik nodded, awash with emotion, not trusting his ability to speak.

Imamu called on her familiar, the three ravens. They burst from the numanen around her neck and set to inspecting the box. Hard beaks tapped and prodded while clever eyes turned this way and that. The birds covered every angle, scratching with talons before finally cawing out a verdict. Black wings turned to smoke and the three of one mind disappeared.

"Cunning," said Imamu. "An old spell put on this box, simple and powerful. The box is tuned to one specific person and will open automatically when this person's vibration is a corresponding frequency."

"Assuming I'm that person, how is this feat accomplished?"

"The ravens couldn't say. Only the caster would know for certain."

"So, I'm on my own."

"Wouldn't be the first time."

Mavrik smiled sheepishly. "I don't know why I expected things to be any different."

"Have faith. Things will work out."

"On that note, any progress regarding this new illness?"

"Not yet."

Mavrik could tell from her posture that she was withholding. He decided not to press the issue, trusting in the wisdom of his teacher. She would tell him when ready.

"Thank you for the lesson," said Mavrik, scooping up the box.

"You still seeing that Roseline?"

He paused, confused. "Sometimes. Why?"

"An old woman's curiosity." She waved a hand, half in farewell, half in annoyance. "Go on your way, you've taken enough of my time this day."

A group of five waited for Mavrik at his strider—three men and two women of varying ages.

"It's not for sale," said Mavrik. "You've stood in the heat for nothing."

"Not for nothing," said the eldest member, a man with grey-silver hair as well as speckles in his cropped beard. "We wait for you."

"Do you require a serviteur?"

"We seek an Omolara."

"I'm the last. My father saw to that when he murdered my mother and died in the process."

The group stiffened. A woman stepped forward, her head and neck wrapped in a thin scarf.

"Ivaylo predicted our current trouble," she said. "He was preparing you for what is coming."

"Oh," said Mavrik, "you must be the so-called Children of the Wolf." He made eye contact with each one of them. "My dear father didn't give a shit about me. I was a tool for his ambitions, just as you are. He destroyed my family."

"I am sorry for your loss," said the bearded leader. "But the facts are undeniable. Your father saw the path that Leadership was taking and desired to divert this future."

"Oberon rejected him for this," said the woman. "Your grandfather has concealed Eldorado and we are suffering because of this."

Mavrik's fingers inched towards the capsule containing gunpowder, his other hand ready to rip free the red bandana tied around his arm. The Ronin would put an end to these bastards and their sermonizing. But not just yet.

"What is Eldorado?"

"Our salvation," said the leader. "An empire, a kingdom, a city, a king, a man."

"Is that all?"

"The Pilgrimage was only the first phase. Eldorado is the culmination."

Mavrik sneered. "I suppose that I'm expected to fulfil this prophecy for you."

"It is your destiny," said the woman.

He'd heard enough. "I'm giving you five seconds to leave. There will be no mercy if you approach me again."

The woman started to speak, but their leader raised a hand to silence her. He nodded, eyes downcast, catching sight of the capsule in Mavrik's hand. They backed away from the strider and sank into the jungle overgrowth.

His interaction with the Children of the Wolf still had Mavrik furious days later. Rouey, exasperated by his friend's behaviour, eventually confronted him.

"If you're so upset, then do something about it!"

"I want nothing to do with them."

"Channel this energy in a different direction. We know these rebels are dubious at best." Rouey raised his hands to ward off Mavrik's glare. "At best!" Undeterred, Rouey pushed on. "Let's find out what Leadership is really up to. Director Ikenna is a creep, but we need to discover if he's a rotten apple or if it's the whole orchard."

Mavrik crossed his arms, unconvinced.

"Team us, remember? How can we decide which way to go if we aren't aware of the options?"

"No one will speak to us willingly."

"Yeah, Leadership are a tight-lipped bunch. We'll have to make them talk."

"I won't use the Politician. Zidati can't be trusted after that stunt he pulled with Caeso."

"What if you wear the mask? The concentration of energy worked with the Sleeper."

Mavrik pulled back his bottom lip, revealing the gap of his missing tooth.

"Mostly worked," Rouey acknowledged. "Well, that leaves us with old fashioned torture, blackmail, or letting this go and moving on to other pursuits."

"Ikenna cheated me out of a sanction. He's got information from the zombie to use for who knows what. I'm not letting this go."

"Too bad the Sleeper won't tell us what the zombie said."

"He's bound to honour a deal. His one redeeming quality."

Rouey ran a hand through his hair. "I don't have any dirt on Leadership, so that leaves torture. You're the serviteur. How dark on the spectrum of grey do you want to go?"

Mavrik's memory flashed to the obsessive passion in his father's eyes, the unyielding ambition. He refused to be like Ivaylo.

"There might be another way," he said, moving to depart.

"That's it?" Rouey called. "I know you're going to see her when you get vague!"

* * *

"You're asking me to break my oath as a neural-counsellor," said Roseline. "To cross a line I said I never would."

Mavrik nodded his assent.

"If you get caught I'll have no choice but to deny any involvement. I'll have to publicly denounce your actions."

"Putting an end to our friendship. I do not risk this lightly."

"Your reputation will take a beating, perhaps irrecoverably. You'll be a social pariah. Is the need so great?"

Mavrik recalled the Hunter's attack that had barely been contained by the Ronin. How to explain?

"I don't have time to wait. Besides, the world only tolerates me as it is."

She saw the burden he carried, sensing the barriers in his words said and withheld.

"Okay," she said, "but now you owe me."

"I will not fail."

Despite their decision to collaborate, Mavrik felt the distance between them widening. First lovers, then friends, and now co-conspirators; an aspect of his Self wept at this development.

* * *

The clinic where Roseline was employed seemed busier than ever, filled by patients seeking to heal their psychological wounds from the quake as well as a growing number of those related to the mysterious new illness. Neural-counselling offered mind-body strategies to promote healing, bridging technology and psychology into a single practice. Mavrik considered this discipline to border on his own, as it utilized technical tools and language to encourage energy to flow intentionally.

A patient linked their neural network to nodes, creating a digital space for their waking mind to communicate with their subconscious. A counsellor, like Roseline, helped the individual to navigate this unfamiliar environment. Considerable trust was required by the patient during this state of vulnerability. This is where Mavrik would make his move.

In their time together, Roseline had let slip some information about her work that had left her feeling disturbed. A member of Leadership—she hadn't given a name—came to the clinic each week, and always conducted his session alone. She suspected that he was using the technology to indulge in personal fantasies. Patients had tried this before in her sessions and her guiding touch brought them back to the task at hand. This particular patient's social status made him beyond reproach. Lately, the frequency of his visits had increased, occupying valuable time with the technology.

Roseline sneaked Mavrik into the office, hiding him behind a desk. The room was inviting but impersonal, a warm sort of neutral. She set the nodes on the table in preparation for her next patient. Mavrik heard the steps of someone entering the room.

"Director Ikenna," said Roseline, "I'll be back for you in an hour."

"Make it two."

"That is quite long for a person to be plugged in on their own."

"I've become adept at using the technology."

"There are other patients who need—"

"They will be seen in due time. Need I remind you that the agency I oversee is the primary funder of this clinic?"

"Be that as it may, two hours alone may pull you so deep that you won't be able to find the surface. Patient health and safety are my primary concerns."

"Worried about losing your certification due to malpractice? Fine. I'll only do an hour and half."

The Director's harsh, authoritarian tone brooked no rebuttal. Roseline exited and shut the door. Ikenna locked it, then settled into a chair, sighing as he slipped the nodes over his head. Mavrik emerged from behind the desk, taking Roseline's chair and observing the rapid twitching of Ikenna's closed eyes.

Mavrik smiled, thin and cruel, he hadn't dreamed for this good fortune. Fate seemed to have a twisted sense of humour. He picked up his own set of nodes connected to the central device. *Say nothing,* had been Roseline's advice. *Be attuned to your emotions. Remain objective.* Mavrik attached the nodes, his doorway into Ikenna's mind.

Electricity tingled at his temples and the sensation of his body disappeared. There was a feeling of tremendous speed, movement in multiple directions at once, then his feet felt supported by solid ground.

He was in a city on Kalubon; the humid heat and sky identical to those Mavrik had known his entire life. The city below—he viewed the scene from on high even though he felt level with the architecture—was like that of a place half-imagined, or half-remembered. Some details were distinct and others barely visible. The central structure was immediately recognizable as the tower where Leadership convened. An unsettling realization crept over Mavrik, akin to looking into a mirror and seeing a different face; he was in a Siridea without the Dome. The sight was unnerving in a way he never could have anticipated, the absence peeling back his complacency. A massive shadow fell over the city, bringing with it an ominous gravitas. An

Alliance starship glided above, completely obscuring Siridea.

One area shimmered in the shadow, somehow catching the darkness and reflecting it as light. Mavrik squinted at this distant structure that he did not recognize. A few steps swallowed the separation, placing him at the base of a four-story black pyramid. He shivered, chilled by the freeze emanating from the surface. Wisps of cold lifted from smooth panels, curling in on themselves and rolling down the slope.

Ikenna's shout echoed from inside and Mavrik watched himself enter the pyramid. This other him walked with head bowed and wrists shackled.

"What the fuck," he said.

The world wobbled at his utterance, vibrating like a triggered alarm system. Ikenna's voice came again, angry this time. Smaller craft burst out of the Alliance starship, ripping overtop the city like swarming insects. Mavrik backed away from the pyramid, right hand instinctively reaching for his chain of numanens. His finger touched Chikere's flute and the familiar streamed into existence within this digital unconscious.

"How…what…" Mavrik stammered.

The Satyr appeared beside him, glowering at the pyramid. "Foul splinter!"

The naked man roared, his eyes flaming red, body tensed and ready to tear the edifice apart piece by piece.

"Stop," said Mavrik.

Chikere faced him and they were equally surprised to be eye to eye. A ship buzzed the capstone, already circling back around. Mavrik felt Ikenna's anger all around him.

He raised two fingers to his temple, pressing hard. "Discontinue."

A rush like being pulled into the sky surrounded Mavrik.

He was back in Roseline's office. He ripped off the nodes and bolted, desperate to get clear before Ikenna followed.

The door wouldn't open. He reefed on the handle until realizing to twist the locking mechanism. Mavrik paused, the door could only be locked from inside. If he left things as they were, then Ikenna would know that Roseline had betrayed the Director's trust. Reluctantly, Mavrik put the wooden mask on his face and began tapping pressure points on his arms, chest, and throat. He spoke swiftly in kallikrates and gripped the gold coin to call forth the Politician.

"Persuade the man in this room that the machine malfunctioned," said Mavrik. "Convince Director Ikenna that he is needed elsewhere for important business."

Zidati chuckled, a smug expression appearing overtop of the mask.

Zidati checked his cufflinks, softly tutting to himself as if amused by his own thoughts. The other stirred in the chair, awakening and removing the headset. Zidati sensed the concealed rage bubbling out of the man, the urge to place blame. He sprang into action before the other, knowing intimately the power inherent to the person who directed the flow of conversation.

"Esteemed Director," said Zidati, adopting an expression of concern. "Our systems detected a malfunction in the machine and I rushed in to check on your well-being. I apologize for interrupting, but I would do so again if it ensured your safety."

The Director's glare fractured for an instant, his gaze dropping to the device. "The session was quite unusual."

Zidati smiled, spreading his hands graciously. "A common report in such circumstances. You did well to recognize this abnormality and pull yourself out before any damage occurred."

Fear split the Director's remaining anger. "Have that machine given a full diagnostic." Suspicion sprouted out the awareness of mortality. "Where is Roseline?"

Zidati sighed with world-weariness, shaking his head in disbelief. "This place never rests. The needs are many and the hands always too few. Busy, busy." He stepped aside, subtly gesturing to the open door. "Surely, an important man such as yourself understands this responsibility?"

Ikenna straightened, adjusting his collar. "Indeed. I must be going. Much to be done."

Zidati stepped further back, using his hands to direct a current of energy toward the doorway. "Thank you for taking time out of your busy day to visit. I assure you that the next session will be more enjoyable."

The Director started walking, a frown creasing his forehead. He seemed as though he wanted to say something, but was having difficulty completing the thought. He was out the door before internal analysis could begin and his confusion bloomed once in the hall. Not wishing to appear indecisive, Ikenna nodded in affirmation to nothing and no one, then continued.

Zidati grinned, pleased as a spoiled feline. "You need me," he said to the body that he rode. "See how your morals and pride melt away in your desperation?"

His form flickered, shifting into smoke.

"Until the next time," said Zidati, disappearing into the coin.

Mavrik came back into his Self. He tucked the mask into a pocket and slipped out the staff entrance that Roseline had shown him. Excited questions buffeted his mind as he ran, but this excitement orbited an icy core of fear, a remnant of Ikenna's mind imparted into him. The black pyramid. An

Alliance starship. Dread, predatory and inevitable, smothered the serviteur's questions.

* * *

Mavrik poured a tall glass of homebrew, needing to stop his hands from trembling.

A noisy buzzer signalling the entrance of a patron interrupted his solitude. He reluctantly went to greet this person, feeling the weight of obligation grow heavier with each step.

"Serviteur," said a woman.

Probably someone's mother. Wife or daughter or mistress. Mavrik didn't care.

"Please," she said. "I need—"

"Leave."

She paused, pretending to not have heard him. "My—"

"I can't help you."

"I can pay."

"Not about the money."

"Social tokens, then." Her face hardened in grim determination. "I will transfer them to you."

"That's illegal." Mavrik smiled, sad and pityingly. "Do I seem so desperate?"

"It is I who am desperate. I will do anything."

He snorted. "That's just it. You won't. I'm the one who must commit the act. Not you."

She tried to speak but nothing came out.

"Go," he said, already turning away.

He left her standing there, resolute even as her last-ditch plan disintegrated. Mavrik proceeded to get staggeringly drunk.

. . .

Cold wind caressed his bare skin like the hands of a selfish lover, each graceful fingertip stealing a little more warmth. Mavrik shivered, curling into a tight ball around the obsidian mirror. The numanen was pressed to his stomach, clutched by both hands in a death grip. A particularly violent shiver startled him out of sleep. His tired mind witnessed an impossibly large moon, pale as bone. Bizarre, human sized plants covered with thorns inhabited the sandy landscape. A figure watched him in the moonlight.

The Ronin raised a finger to his lips for silence. Wary eyes scanned the periphery; a hand resting on the handle of a revolver. Mavrik came to his feet, still holding the mirror.

They were outside, seemingly in the middle of nowhere. Mavrik listened to the wind, feeling it rattle through him, speaking in a tongue meant for cold-blooded beings.

"You brought something," said the Ronin.

Mavrik caught his reflection in the gifted numanen.

"Say nothing," said the Ronin. "Can't take any chances."

Mavrik looked for sign of the Hunter, seeing only distance and loneliness. The apparition must have escaped the previous encounter. The Ronin appeared no worse for wear.

"There's a hunger inside that mirror," said the gunfighter. "I can perceive the hint of it in this phantom light."

Mavrik raised it level with the moon; dark and smooth as the other was bright and weathered. The object didn't reflect the shine, instead it seemed to swallow it up. His fingers turned bitter cold, but strangely, he felt no pain.

"Ain't natural," said the Ronin.

Suddenly, the mirror exploded in a loud bang. Mavrik flinched. The Ronin set his gun back in its holster.

Mavrik swore loudly.

He was on the floor in the back room of his office. The

obsidian mirror was scattered into a thousand shards all around him.

* * *

Rouey turned on the light in Mavrik's room.

"How many witches does it take to drink all of my beer?"

Mavrik buried his face in a pillow.

"Just one," said Rouey. "Which is the same number of patrons who won't leave my office."

"She's still here?"

"Nekane is adamant about securing your services. She's stopped speaking to me and I have no intention of wrestling her out the door." Rouey turned the light off and on repeatedly. "Your problem to solve. I need to start a new batch of homebrew."

Mavrik rolled out of bed, sure that he'd scare her off after a glance at his haggardness. Nekane observed his entrance from the lone chair in the entry room.

"Good," she said. "You look ready to see what I have to show you."

"And what's that?"

"Hopelessness." She stood, adjusting a scarf around her neck and shoulders. "My family is suffering from an illness. They're all dying."

Pain, raw and visceral, thrummed through Mavrik. "They have given up." He viewed her again, noting the pride in her posture. "But you haven't."

"I must be brave for them."

An aspect inside of her slid, rattling her appearance of strength. Doubt. He watched her push back and turn the tide before it transformed into fear.

"Okay," he said. "Let's go."

"Go wash up." She smiled in motherly concern. "Help yourself before you can help others."

Mavrik nodded and took her advice.

An hour later they were approaching her house, two blocks from where the Fortress and its secret resided. Sections of the street were split from the quake. Piles of rubble yet to be cleared. Nekane's place was a narrow two-story, identical to the rest in the neighbourhood.

"They may not even notice your presence," she said. "It's like they are weary of living yet do not know how to die. They eat and move and sometimes speak, but it is a listless existence."

"What have the medics said?"

Nekane huffed. "Nothing useful. Some even claim that my family is faking this."

"What about neural-counselling?"

"Such a process involves active participation. A willingness to heal." She opened the door. "Let your own Self be the judge."

The interior seemed normal enough—clean, all the necessities of daily living available. They found Nekane's husband straightaway, slumped on the couch, staring into the feed of a wall-mounted streamer.

"Hello," said Mavrik.

The other just blinked, his face slack.

"He'll sit like that for hours," said Nekane. "Come."

She led him upstairs and into her son's room. The lights were off and it took a moment for Mavrik to locate the teenager crouched in a corner. The youth muttered nonsense words to himself.

"He'll scream if I turn on the light," said Nekane. "But he won't do anything about it. Just scream and hide."

Movement from behind gave Mavrik a fright, making him jump. An adolescent girl walked by and went downstairs. Nekane sighed and followed. Mavrik closed the bedroom door.

The girl was rummaging through drawers and cupboards that were noticeably empty. She quietly went about this task, paying no mind to being watched.

"She's looking for something sharp," said Nekane. "Has a fascination with blades. I had to hide them."

"Would she use them to harm?"

"I don't know and didn't want to find out."

The girl finished her search and returned to her room upstairs.

"How long have they been like this?"

Nekane's shoulders drooped. "Strangeness started with many families a few weeks before the quake."

Mavrik gently placed his hands on her upper arms. "I will do everything within my power to help them."

Nekane finally broke, an inner cave-in. She pressed into Mavrik's chest and wept. "I'm so tired of being alone."

Mavrik held her while she released some of her sorrow. When she was ready, he let go, and set to accessing the Naga.

Danya vanished into the cross, her frustration lacing the air with an acidic taste. All of her techniques had proven ineffective. Mavrik sat and Nekane brought some water.

"She has passion," said Nekane.

"But no cure."

Mavrik drank the water then called on Chikere.

The Satyr acted almost civilized, for once. Fascinated by the condition of the family members, he went to each one in turn, gazing deep into their eyes. Following these lengthy energetic examinations, he took Nekane's hands in his and wept.

"Too deep," said Chikere. "Their wounds are too deep."

Tears of grief dribbled into his beard until he hung his head in shame and drifted into the numanen.

"He knows love," said Nekane, drying her own eyes.

"But offers no solution."

Mavrik put on the wooden mask and called on Domagoj.

The Sleeper whirled into form, tipping his hat to Nekane.

"Alcohol and tobacco, if you please, madam."

"I have neither."

Anger like fire in the dark holes of his eyes. The light faded and he smiled congenially.

"Then I shall depart."

"Please," she said, pointing to her husband. "Just take a quick look at him."

Domagoj sniffed the air, head tilted, he followed his nose over to the couch. "Intriguing."

He poked and prodded the other and received no feedback. From inside of his hat he procured a long needle, which he jammed into a meaty thigh. No reaction.

"What's this?" he said, waggling his fingers around the needle.

He plucked out the implement and strode over to Nekane.

"Your unfortunate does not have a bodily affliction. He bears a soul-wound."

"What does that mean?"

"It means he is neither here nor there. His soul wanders aimlessly at the crossroads."

"Can you help him? My son and daughter as well?"

"I can help them to make a choice." He tilted his head sympathetically. "And because of your suffering I will do so without any further dealing. Do you accept?"

Nekane closed her eyes and nodded.

"Splendid!"

The sickle appeared in Domagoj's hand. He promptly slashed down at the immobile man on the couch. Nekane shrieked as her husband's head rolled onto the floor.

"He chose," said Domagoj, reverently "Where are the others?"

Nekane froze. Domagoj sniffed the air and raced upstairs. Nekane forced herself to pursue, arriving to see her son's head tumble off.

"A choice made," said Domagoj.

Nekane collapsed to the floor in shock. Domagoj slipped past and into the hall to find a girl staring up at him. Her eyes latched onto the sickle blade.

"There is life in you yet," said the Sleeper.

The girl extended an arm and Domagoj handed her the sickle. She awkwardly hefted it with both hands, then drove the point into her chest. The blade passed through her body and clattered against the floor. Domagoj clapped his hands together in excitement.

"An excellent choice!"

"Mu…muh…mother," said the girl.

Domagoj swept off his hat and bowed, first to the daughter, then to Nekane. "Farewell."


A daughter stumbled into her mother's waiting arms. Mavrik slumped against the wall, listening to Nekane's uncontrollable weeping. He took off the mask and smiled, seeing the daughter returning the embrace. His happiness faded at the scent of fresh blood.

A sense of vertigo overcame him, playing tricks with his vision. He thought he saw a figure at the end of the hall. A man in tattered blue clothing. There came a voice like a roar. The Hunter had found him.

Suddenly alert, Mavrik wrapped his eyes with the red bandana. He snorted the gunpowder and called on the Ronin. The Hunter charged.

Twin revolvers shot at the apparition, emptying both cylinders. The Ronin peered at the empty space. He put the guns away and floated into the shell casing. Mavrik stared at bullet holes in the wall. No sign of any adversary.

"I was sure…"

"Please," said Nekane, covering her daughter like a human shield. "Don't kill us."

"I would never."

"Not you. Your familiars."

Mavrik staggered away, slowly finding his legs as he came to grips with the grim algebra performed in this home: two deaths and one life. But he'd done the seemingly impossible and remedied an incurable illness. This realization brought no joy.

* * *

A person is inclined to avoid questioning their beliefs, and even more so when the inquiry relates to aspects of what and who they think they are. To pry at this doubt is considered an equivalent to certain death, because of an unconscious awareness about a truth inhabiting a person's inner sanctum; the falseness of their certainty. Acknowledging this truth gives it a momentum that is feared to be unstoppable. Power shifts as the question expands.

Mavrik's familiars provided healing and caused harm. He was only a vessel. A serviteur and a witch; a function and a symbol. To all except Roseline, one who knew the man.

"It feels like I'm being punished," said Mavrik. "My intuition has gone silent and I keep smashing into wall after wall."

They sat at her dining table, drinking tea in the early morning.

"Do you know why we never became a couple?"

"I wasn't sure that's something you wanted."

"We only talk about you. Mavrik's problems suck all the oxygen out of the room." Roseline brushed a strand of hair behind her ear. "I'm a neural-counsellor, but only during sessions, not in my personal life."

"I'm sorry."

He pushed back the chair to leave, but she stopped him with an outstretched hand.

"You've been out of balance for a long time," she said. "I never held this against you and I don't plan to start."

"That's still talking about me. What do you want to talk about?"

"Liberation. A Kalubon that has transcended the current paradigm. The split between witches and Leadership, Anima and technology, have reached a tipping point. The signs are all around us."

Mavrik's eyes widened. "I had no idea you were this passionate about societal issues."

"I'm doing my part to support others in healing, but the fracture is increasing exponentially. I fear it's too little too late."

Mavrik didn't mention his discovery about the illness. He bottled his anxiety regarding the boldness of the Hunter, keeping silent the dread instilled by his intrusion into Ikenna's mind. Roseline had opened up and he would be honourable, keeping the conversation about her.

"What does this transcendent Kalubon look like?"

She looked away, suddenly bashful. "Like Eldorado. A place of unity, abundance, and fulfillment."

"Where did you learn that name?"

"You already know, if you're asking the question."

Mavrik pulled his hand away. His gratitude for her years of compassion towards him nearly overpowered by his rising anger.

"I want to save this world and its people," said Roseline. "I can help you let go of the anchors holding you down."

"I'm just an investment. Save me so I can save everyone."

"Not everyone has the same gifts of Anima."

"Gifts," Mavrik scowled. "You know better than anyone what a curse they can be."

"I know you and I share a similar dream, even if you won't say so. Together we can make it into reality."

"This *we* includes Ivaylo. You are his tool. I won't be your puppet."

"You owe me." She smacked the table with an open palm. "I took a huge risk giving you access to Director Ikenna at the clinic."

"Not all risk is rewarded."

He pushed away from the table, pausing at the door, accepting that this was the last time he'd visit.

"Mavrik, heal your Self, heal the world."

Heart torn open, he slammed the door and kept walking.

Mavrik finished retelling the events of Nekane's house, excluding the bit about the Hunter. He said nothing regarding his interaction with Roseline.

"This is it," said Rouey. "The Sleeper's remedy will gain you the social tokens necessary to move into the upper echelon."

"Two of the clients were decapitated."

"Domagoj's methods are a touch macabre, but we can spin that." Rouey frowned. "Somehow."

Rouey's streamer whirred to life, flashing an emergency

signal. He activated the message, making it visible by hologram. *Volcanic activity in the Northwest has destroyed the city of Bridh and ash threatens to engulf the surrounding area.*

"That's Kalubon's second largest city," said Rouey. "All those people. Gone."

"Geologic sensors should have given an evacuation warning. Same with the quake here."

"These aren't isolated incidents; this is a pattern."

"Maybe I'm supposed to go to Bridh," said Mavrik. "Diviner told me that a great journey approaches."

"Travel halfway around the globe to see a mass graveyard?"

Mavrik tossed up his hands in frustration. "Well, I don't know what else to do!"

"Go see your teacher. Maybe she has some Anima wisdom to bestow."

"A smack upside the head is more likely."

"Whatever works." Rouey nodded at the streamer. "I'm going to keep watching. Leadership will be making a statement."

The thought of Ikenna made Mavrik angrier. He activated the strider and raced out of the city.

No ravens to mark his arrival. Only echo and shadow occupied Imamu's cave. Her teapot lay on its side in a damp circle on the rug. Items were scattered on the floor, knocked over and left where they'd fallen. The hairs on Mavrik's neck prickled. No Imamu and a scene of struggle. He grabbed the goat skin drum and beater and started hammering out a fast rhythm.

Vapour poured out of the flute, encircling Mavrik's body, replacing clothing with flesh. Chikere flexed his muscles.

"Imamu, my teacher, has been taken," said Mavrik. "Track her."

"The fiends must be particularly vile if they withstood her club."

Chikere crouched on the rug, sniffing like an animal. He crawled on hands and feet, surveying the entirety of the cave. Strong fingers and toes gripped the rock wall to hold1 him in place horizontally.

"Curious," he said. "She knew at least one of them."

He leapt off the wall, striding to the cave entrance, the mingling scents rolling in his nostrils. There could be no escape! The Satyr bolted down the path, bare toes pounding on the jungle turf.

Chikere relished the chase, his heart beating joyfully, his form a blur against the greens and browns. Such fools were these kidnappers! They moved like a youth drunk on its first cup of wine, leaving behind markings he could have followed in the dark.

The jungle was roaring in his ears. The sensation of life filled him up. Onward he ran, teeth bared in a mad grin.

And then the trail vanished into thin air. Chikere skidded to a stop. He prowled in concentric circles, scanning up and down, his energy merging with the landscape. His feet hardened and darkened, transitioning into split hooves. The hair on his legs grew thicker.

"Where have you gone?" he whispered, singing the phrase over and over.

He pounced on a stone jutting out of the fallen leaves. Rough fingers scoured the hard surface, flicking open a section at the top. A single button was set into the stone.

"Found you!"

Chikere pressed the button, laughing in unrestrained delight as an elevator lifted out of the ground. His blue eyes were streaked with lightning. The tips of horns appeared in his curly head of hair. The Satyr stepped onto the elevator, descending into a jungle underworld. His chase became a hunt.

The elevator touched down within an underground cave illumined by electric lights. Rock walls, narrow like a hallway, ended at a closed metal door, guarded by a pair of men holding weapons.

"Villains," said Chikere, his voice skittering across the stone.

"The fuck?"

The Satyr stepped from the elevator, leaping the distance before the guards could aim their firearms. He gripped a man in each hand, hurling them into the ceiling. The men crashed to the ground and he brought his fists down on them. Chikere stepped to the door—a sheet of thick steel locked from inside.

He sang to the stone around the doorframe, flattering its quality and giving his respects. The stone awakened, confused at first, and then pleased with this respectful greeting. He made a request of the stone, a simple and easy asking of such a noble mineral. The stone granted its blessing. Chikere plunged his fingers into the stone adjacent to the door, digging free a space to get his hands in, then his forearms all the way to his shoulders. Teeth clenched, he pulled against the steel.

The door gave way, just a bit, but that was all he needed. Curling horns descended past his ears. Chikere redoubled his effort and the frame bent. He elbowed his way through the gap. The Satyr whooped in ecstasy; he was in.

Shouting and shots rang out all around like chaotic music. Chikere attacked, swift and unrelenting as a thundercloud in its fury. He crumpled villain after villain. Screams and blood and the thrill of physicality. Two scents, two women, slowed his rampage.

The teacher and the lover.

Mavrik's consciousness swam towards the surface. The Satyr's hold didn't want to release. The serviteur summoned the force of his willpower.

"Your mission is complete!"

Chikere's inhuman form disintegrated as he acknowledged the witch. Mavrik stumbled, dropping to a knee, face ashen and dripping a cold sweat. He didn't want to look up, didn't want to believe what was in front of him.

"I'll kill her if you take another step," said Roseline, firearm pressed into Imamu's back.

Imamu's lip was bloodied and her eyes tired. She seemed more upset about her student's condition than her own situation.

"They demanded a reading from Diviner," said Imamu, "then tried to beat the future out of me when I refused. Ha!"

"How did we come to this?" asked Mavrik, face downcast.

He stood, struggling to do so under his own power. Roseline's face was grim with determination. Imamu looked bored.

"Get her to call on Diviner and afterwards we can all go our separate ways," said Roseline.

"No," said Mavrik.

"That's the student I trained," said Imamu.

Roseline shifted the firearm to Mavrik's chest. "Fine. Call on Diviner or I shoot."

Imamu's confidence wavered. Mavrik took a step closer and Roseline swore.

"I'll do it!" her voice carrying a frantic pitch. She blinked, confused and angry. "Stop that."

"Stop what?"

"No familiars."

"I'm not doing anything."

"I see it too," said Imamu. "A being that's more beast than man, with smoke rising from its eyes."

"Stop it!" Roseline's anger was slipping into fear.

A guttural growl crawled around them, alternating between near and far. Mavrik sighed, feeling beaten, not seeing a way out of this. Roseline tracked with the firearm, moving its line of sight off Mavrik's chest. Imamu reached back with both hands, fighting with Roseline for control of the weapon.

Three screeching ravens flocked around the women, pecking and scratching at Roseline. She screamed, squeezing the trigger. Multiple shots let loose, one ripping into Imamu. The elderly witch fell; her birds diving on Roseline, viciously attacking the face and neck. Roseline got off a few more shots before dropping, never to move again.

Cruel laughter echoed. The Hunter was enjoying this outcome. Mavrik spun, looking for the apparition, but the ghoul had departed. Imamu coughed, wet with blood. He rushed to her side.

"...you...beast..." Imamu choked out.

She tried to speak again, but all that came out was a rattling wheeze. The brightness in her eyes faded and she went still.

Mavrik scooped up Imamu's body, unnerved by how small she felt, this person who'd loomed so large in his life. He shambled to the elevator on numb legs, his mind screaming, his soul ripped to shreds.

Kallikrates thrummed out of his throat upon emerging on the surface. The beautiful power twisting language around energy, shaping words capable of influencing physical form. Mavrik spoke the death rites for his departed teacher. He set her down in a ray of sunlight splitting the canopy. Palms hovering over Imamu's body, he gave himself to the fluid words of potent meaning.

He had no thought or intent, fuelled by a profound emptiness. Words built on each other, instinctively creating pattern beyond comprehension. Golden threads appeared on Imamu, gradually coalescing into a shimmering sheet. Mavrik could no longer hear the words; he was light and earth, wind and flame. He sensed Anima, felt the grace moving through him, being channeled for his task.

Then he was a boy of ten, peeking into an unknown cave, spying on the woman inside.

"I won't bite if you don't," she'd said.

Mavrik took a monumental first step.

The kallikrates dried up, the last drop falling from his lips. Imamu was radiance. The sheet slowly lowered, taking her body as well. Mavrik kneeled in silence, more alone than he'd ever believed possible. In a trance, he made his way to the strider, the black tentacles steadily returning him home, the world around him as distant as an Alliance planet.

He went straight to the box labeled Eldorado. An object of simple construction and careful lettering. This unexpected gift from his grandfather. Mavrik reached for it, the seal cracking open at his touch.

* * *

Down and down he went in a body that wasn't his own. Mavrik felt like a passenger in someone else's mind. He could see and sense and move, but had no control over any of these functions. Step after countless step he/they descended a spiral staircase made of crystal.

Strange multicolour lights covered the near wall like circuitry. A steady warmth increased the further he/they went. Booted feet, larger than his own, finally stepped off the staircase. The heat was atrocious, sizzling against the exterior of the encasing suit he/they wore.

The other him spoke kallikrates; a spell Mavrik had never encountered. Language and energy and environment blended. Intention remained concealed from Mavrik's awareness. He/they focused power on a mechanical orb resting on a narrow pedestal. Lines of energy materialized from the cardinal directions to converge within the orb. He set hands that were not his own on this centering object.

Excruciating pain consumed him. Mavrik would have passed out, but this other was stronger than he. The energetic lines reshaped into a dodecahedron: twelve sides, twenty points, thirty edges and 6480 degrees. Soul and mind and physical separated, only in contact by the thinnest of threads. The orb pulled at these different aspects, drawing them into itself. Terror, pure and instinctual, clawed at Mavrik's mind. Every part of him would be consumed by the orb and he was powerless to change it.

The flow of kallikrates ceased and with its going the lines of energy closed. A small green light on the orb flared to life. Mavrik could feel the missing parts of his Self and with this realization came despair. Because he knew, in his heart of hearts, that this wasn't the first time that he/they had gone through this procedure, and it wouldn't be the last. He/they would heal, just enough, and this act would be repeated. An endless torment.

Weary feet began the long climb.

* * *

Mavrik sat in a chair, bare feet on the table, staring at the unsealed box. Afraid to look inside.

He was reeling, his sense of reality tenuous. Imamu's death. Roseline's betrayal. Pursuit by the Hunter. An experience where *he* was the one doing the possessing. And that wasn't even counting the bullshit inside of Ikenna's mind, the natural disasters ravaging Kalubon, or the lurking threat of a mysterious illness. In spite of everything, here he sat with the secret to Eldorado available.

The Children of the Wolf wanted this more than anything. Oberon had hidden it away, attuning the box to Mavrik. Questions drifted behind his eyes, dissipating before they could trickle down to his throat. Rouey entered, startling Mavrik into attention.

"Leadership says everything is fine," said Rouey. "Making claims of newly developed tech that will solve all of our worries." He dropped onto the couch. "A bunch of pandering and denial. Can't admit there's a problem, but if there is, then they just happen to have a solution. Or will, sometime in the future."

"Yeah, yeah…"

"Imamu say something that got you rattled?"

"She said…I'm not sure what sure what she said"

Rouey sat upright. "What's wrong?"

Mavrik shared everything, spilling his guts, needing to stop and start on several occasions.

"The worst part is that I sort of feel grateful," said Mavrik. He pointed to the box. "It's open."

"Have you?"

Mavrik shook his head.

"Should we?"

A shrug to say, probably.

The buzzer sounded, signifying the entrance of a patron.

"I'll get rid of them," said Rouey.

He poked his head in a few moments later, face tight with shock, motioning for Mavrik to join him. Something about the expression, a quality of witnessing the sublime, pulled the reluctant witch to his feet.

Nekane and her daughter stood in the office entry. The

girl half hid behind her mother's leg as Nekane practically glowed with happiness.

"Aisha wishes to speak with you," said Nekane, nudging the girl forward.

Aisha brushed away a lock of dark hair partially covering her face. Mavrik gasped at the abundance of life emanating out of those brown, almond-shaped eyes.

"Thank you," she said. "Thank you for helping me find my Self."

Nekane beamed, squeezing her daughter's hand tightly. Mavrik was speechless.

"Her soul-wound has been healed," said Nekane. "This is what your familiar called it. I am forever grateful."

Mavrik still didn't know how to respond. He felt faint from the joy within Nekane's smile, the vitality of young Aisha.

"Just part of the job," said Rouey, slapping Mavrik's shoulder.

He placed an open hand overtop the numanens, over his heart, and bowed his head with eyes shut. They were gone when he looked up.

"Today has given me a lot to process," said Rouey. "I'm not ready for whatever's in the box."

"It's waited this long. It can wait a little more."


Prevailing winds created a sinister morning, carrying ash from the eruption in Bridh. Slate-grey clouds smothered a normally brilliant blue sky. Ashy flakes drifted, landing delicately and piling heavily. A scent of sulfur itched inside of nostrils, scratching at a dormant piece of physiology; the animal need for survival.

Those who had the option remained indoors, while others hurried between locations with eyes straight ahead, trying, and failing, to ignore this omen. A rabble outside built into a rumble moving towards the Dome, the streets filling with masked protestors. The Children of the Wolf had officially come out of hiding, empowered by substantial support from the people.

Mavrik wondered if his raid on their hideout had helped instigate this uprising. The roaring mob surged past the nondescript building labeled '6.' Rouey tossed a mask over and they followed at the tail-end.

Ash stomped by thousands of boots pressed between Mavrik's toes as hard-packed grit. Countless flakes descended, thinning the sunlight. Ahead, came a collective snarl as the head of the snake met resistance. A kinetic clash of conflict rippled down the mass of protestors. In the near distance, just visible through the falling ash, stood the Dome, its upper curve receding into a grey smear.

"We should get out of here while we still can," said Rouey.

Screaming and shouting trickled overtop of the mob as the fighting intensified. Mavrik felt a change in the air pressure, like a massive inhalation. His ribcage squeezed in on itself. Bursts of crimson fire spewed from multiple spots on the Dome. A concussive blast swept over all sound, stirring up a maelstrom of ash. Huge sections of the Dome fell inwards.

People were screaming, the hostility instantly transforming into panic. Individuals scrambled to escape, now fighting to return the way they'd come. Meanwhile, the Dome burned, liquid fire eating away at Kalubon's iconic structure. Mavrik and Rouey ran to stay ahead of the frightened horde.

They ducked inside the office, shaking off dust and disorder.

"Those were explosions," said Rouey, ripping his mask aside. "That was planned."

"The rebels are going to be annihilated for this, whether they're guilty or not."

"Not if I can help it," said a man's voice.

Mavrik and Rouey stopped in the entry, staring down the barrels of multiple firearms. The intruders wore masks and hoods, leaving only their eyes visible. One held the box in the crook of an arm, the golden letters flashing.

Tase-jolts coursed through Mavrik's body, dropping him to the floor. Firm hands tied his hands behind his back, forcefully hoisting him to his feet and shoving him into the chaos outside.

* * *

Arcs of pain tightened and strained various areas of Mavrik's body, stalling his breath for long heartbeats, until finally releasing. When these electric rivulets eventually faded he noticed he was on his knees in a bare room, surrounded by masked individuals.

"Where's Rouey?"

"Left him thrashing on the floor," said the leader, the same bearded man who'd approached Mavrik with the Children of the Wolf in the jungle. "He'll be waking up soon enough."

They set the box in front of him. The secret that had consumed his family. He would pretend to play their game and when his hands were free he'd access the Ronin, then—

A set of hands lifted the chain of numanens from around Mavrik's neck.

"Bastards," Mavrik growled. "I need those."

"I'll be the judge of that," said the leader.

They untied him and he rubbed at aching wrists. His gaze was inexorably drawn to the box, the mystery of Eldorado becoming undeniable. A grand truth must be inside, a reason for all of this suffering and death.

The leader motioned with his weapon. "Get to it."

Mavrik, capitulating to fate, reached for the box.

The door burst open and the room turned into a firestorm.

Spec-ops in reflective helmets shot the rebels. Bodies dropped around a kneeling witch in four seconds of carnage. Mavrik dove for his numanens. A hard boot cracked into his chest, knocking him back; another pinning him to the floor. There came a clink and rattle of his chain being picked up.

"Stand down," said a familiar, infuriating voice.

The boot was removed and Director Ikenna stepped into view, holding the numanens in one hand and the box in the other.

"Don't worry," said Ikenna. "You will be encouraged to continue." He looked at the drab, plain walls. "But in a place more fitting for one of your kind."

He exited and spec-ops followed his lead, ushering Mavrik forward in a tight circle. They marched down the street, an island of calm amidst the turmoil, a pack of predators best avoided. A chill wind whipped ash into spirals, the tropical warmth subdued by a deepening separation from the sun. Mavrik soon recognized the district, guessing where they were going, his fury shifting to a controlled cold; the black walls of the Fortress appearing against the gloom.

A full street over, they directed Mavrik into a business entrance, jostling him between their armoured bodies inside a tube-like elevator, and descending to reach a smooth-walled tunnel.

"I knew it," Mavrik mumbled.

Well-lit and straight as a needle, the tunnel led them into the Fortress. Sounds of fabrication came from above. The group continued their descent, taking a metal staircase to a lower level, corkscrewing down to a more confined space. The walls were covered in complex circuitry and appeared to be arranged as an inverted pyramid. Ikenna waited at the bottom, standing beside a pedestal in the otherwise empty area.

"Welcome," he said, "I'm glad you were able to join us."

He wore the serviteur's chain around his neck.

Mavrik lunged. A blow between his shoulder blades rocked him. Another to a thigh dropping him to a knee.

"You have no respect for anything," said Mavrik, pushing himself to stand.

"Inaccurate," said Ikenna, nodding for the spec-ops to leave.

He kept a firearm trained on the witch as the others clomped up the stairs.

"I respect progress," said the Director. "I respect the ambition to seize opportunity." He observed with a disconcerting detachment. "I respect change enough to be the person to make it happen."

"The rebels are forcing their own agenda."

"Are you referring to the Dome?" Ikenna smirked. "Who do you think seeded that idea within their ranks?" His humour expanded at Mavrik's obvious confusion. "But why? I'm Leadership? While the rest of Council is struggling with the fallout, I will surpass them." He set the box on the pedestal. "With this."

"I won't help you."

"You're a ghost of a former time, but you have one more task."

The phrase jogged Mavrik's memory: a boy had also called him a ghost, a boy who'd said the time of witches was ending, a boy with a cough.

"I met your son," said Mavrik. "He seemed ill."

Ikenna's smugness drooped. Sadness welled to the brink. He pushed it back down.

"It's gotten worse then," said Mavrik. "He's lost to you, isn't he?"

"Enough tricks," Ikenna spat.

"He has a soul-wound. I can cure it."

Rage flared in Ikenna's eyes. "Because you're an all-powerful Omolara?" His finger slid back and forth on the trigger of the firearm. "Your family is nothing but cheats and liars." He jabbed emphatically with the weapon. "You didn't earn the name Two Handed Hoarder, you inherited it. Oberon stole from his twin brother, *my* grandfather, in order to become a hero."

"You're crazy. Oberon's brother never returned from Pilgrimage."

"He did. Without his ability to access Anima. Somewhere along the journey your grandfather betrayed mine and took his power."

"The sacred cannot be stolen. Your ancestor must have been deemed unworthy." He looked long and hard at Ikenna. "And shit flows downhill."

"Opportunity wasn't just *given* to me, I've had to make it happen for my own Self."

Mavrik almost laughed—or cried—genuinely impressed at the creativity of his family curse. Ikenna opened the lid of the box.

Darkness, rich and textured, enveloped everything as it subsumed existence. Mavrik might have fallen if he'd had any sense of where he was. Movement started within the darkness, an inexorable spin. Forward and back, outward and inward; all direction simultaneously. Once again, his lack of bodily sensation saved him, this time from nausea. With the spinning came light, thin streaks growing into a burning sphere.

Blindingly bright and radiating energy, the sphere split into two. Two became three in the shape of a triangle. Three more spheres formed in a line below, creating the appearance of a square attached to the triangular top. A final ball of light manifested to the side like a tail or handle. Seven dazzling lights filled Mavrik's awareness, concentrating the dark-spin.

"I know this," he whispered.

"The Shepherd King constellation," said Ikenna. "The zombie said to target Errai, the star atop the crown."

Mavrik's gaze was drawn to the star at the upper point of the triangle. Kallikrates began bubbling up inside of him as if transplanted by Errai. He looked away, unwilling to collude with Ikenna's ambitions.

A new player surged into the celestial drama, powered by the circuitry along the walls of the inverted pyramid. Crackling energetic lines shot out from the four cardinal directions, piercing Mavrik's chest.

He gasped in shock, expecting pain, yet feeling bliss. The star of Errai filled his vision, its light overwhelming his mind. Kallikrates gushed forth, attaching to the moving darkness of the constellation. Language gripped the spin like fingers on a handle. Mavrik and kallikrates were entwined; he could feel every detail of the handle; sense the limitless possibility on the other side. A threshold revealed its design.

He put his whole hand into the constellation and twisted his wrist.

# PART II
# OF MATTERS IMMATERIAL

It's been said that all things emerged from nothing, and that everything is actually an illusion. Yet within all this nothing is an ineffable *something*. Most take the status of their existence as proof of something. Some say this *something* is love. A human needs this paradox, this intuitively known fusion of duality, just as a person needs love, because it's easier to love what is known. Entering the constellation didn't give Mavrik insight into inscrutable truths, but with a simple hand motion he instantly destroyed all the concepts he'd believed to be true.

He joined a space of synthesis, of union, of enmeshed paradox. His mind broke. Emotions dissolved. Body long gone. Mavrik wasn't.

And then, remarkably, perhaps inevitably, he was. Once again. He felt *something*.

Mavrik blinked. A blisteringly red sun crested the horizon—shifting solar currents visible inside of the sphere. The sky had a golden cast and the clouds a soft flaxen that glittered. Wind, dry and insistent, tugged at his clothing. Bare feet were planted on parched grassland. Awareness pushed its way inside like an uninvited guest.

"I'm here," he said, looking at the barren landscape. "Wherever this is."

No sign of Ikenna. No sign of anything. He touched the empty space where his chain of numanens had hung for years. On his own. Truly.

Footprints baked into the soil led away from his position. The individual who'd made them had also been barefoot. Mavrik set a foot inside the nearest print; an exact match. He gasped and withdrew. A questioning look over his shoulder, but no, the footprints started here, where he stood. The sun remained in its position astride the horizon, unmoving. A gust of wind slammed into his back, shuffling him forward. Mavrik couldn't shake the sense of intention he felt in the shove.

He started walking, keeping parallel to the other tracks, which were a dead ringer for his own stride.

"Fuck this," he said, turning around and going in the opposite direction.

Step after step Mavrik broke new ground, occasionally glancing back at a sun that wouldn't rise. A chill wind buffeted his advance, so he tilted his head down and leaned into it, locked into a battle of wills. Whistling in his ears and rattling his braids, but lacking any real teeth, the wind soon subsided. Mavrik brushed off this small victory and continued his trek into nowhere, targeting a dark spot against the horizon.

The spot of interest steadily grew into a tall, wizened tree that seemed long dead. Smooth branches twisted into an empty crown. A frayed rope hung from the lowest branch, its end fashioned into a noose. Mavrik gazed at the symbol, trying to parse its meaning.

"Well, well, look who it is," said a man, stepping out from behind the tree.

He wore a hat like the Ronin, his face stained with dust and sweat. Revolvers on each hip and a long knife hitched to his belt.

"I think you've mistaken me for someone else," said Mavrik. "We've never met."

The other spat, stained yellow by tobacco. "Now that's just plain rude, not remembering a man you've killed." He sucked at his teeth. "The name's Roy Westin, seeing as you forgot."

A crunching of multiple boots spun Mavrik around to see two additional men step into view. One wore a huge flat-brimmed hat and a bandolier crossing his chest from shoulder to hip. The other had a neckerchief below a coarse beard, opting for a smaller, rounded hat.

"Got Mexi and Jonesy here too," said Westin. "The whole gang is back together."

Jonesy's shotgun was already out, slung at the hip with both hands. Mexi grinned, withdrawing a machete.

"I'm not who you think I am," said Mavrik, his hand moving instinctively for the red bandana tied around his arm. The lightness on his collarbone stopping the motion.

Westin's icy blue eyes appraised Mavrik's lack of weaponry. "You look damn near naked without your guns. Almost doesn't seem fair. Almost."

Out of habit, Mavrik spoke in kallikrates, but nothing came. The beautiful power was gone.

Mexi lunged, bashing Mavrik in the head with the machete handle. Mavrik dropped. Westin started in on him with kicks from his pointed boots. Mavrik winced as the blows shuddered into him, his forehead bleeding into the dirt. Jonesy hefted him up and walk-carried him over to the rope, slipping the noose around Mavrik's neck. Rough fibers scuffed his skin, the pressure tight on his throat. Jonesy removed his support and Mavrik gagged as the tips of his toes scraped at the ground.

Desperate fingers reached for the noose; stopped by several vicious strikes to the back. Westin and Jonesy stepped into eyesight, the shotgun trained on him once more. Mavrik fought for balance, his feet unable to touch down. Black splotches eclipsed his vision. Panic, urgent and helpless, surged through his veins. Westin smiled, enjoying the show.

A sharp crack split the scene and Mavrik landed unceremoniously, choking for air. Three more blasts then silence. Mavrik tugged loose the rope, sitting up to see three dead bodies around him.

"It's one thing for evil to return," said the Ronin, refilling the chambers of his revolver. "And I can reason why greed won't stay dead." Disgust merged into wonderment as he looked at the corpses. "But incompetence has no right to a second chance. What's the point?"

Mavrik moved unsteadily to his feet, examining the rope that the Ronin's first shot had severed. The dead men were rapidly decaying, their bodies, clothing and all, shrinking and compacting. Three shiny black scorpions with barbed tails scuttled away.

"That ain't right," said the Ronin.

"No," Mavrik said roughly, "but nothing here seems to be."

The Ronin nodded at the tree, which was undergoing a radical transformation. Mavrik scrambled further back, towards the gunfighter, trusting in the familiarity even if he couldn't explain its reason for being.

Green leaves sprouted from every inch of every branch; white flowers with yellow centers interspersing the foliage. An intoxicating scent of life wafted from the tree, displacing the cloud of fear created by Mavrik's near demise, and overcorrecting the blandness of the landscape. The flowers elongated into the graceful necks of white swans, their wings spreading wide and radiating light. A flock lifted from the bough, brilliant against the gold sheen of the sky. Leaves curled and dried on the branches until slowly descending to the earth. The tree was once more as Mavrik had found it.

"Come on, Tasunka," said the Ronin. "Let's move on."

"They thought I was you," said Mavrik, falling in beside the psychopomp.

"Westin's crew never struck me as the brightest, but they weren't blind."

"You killed them already. Before I was involved."

A grunt of acknowledgement.

"How is that possible?"

"Don't know. Most of my memory must have run off with my name."

Mavrik sighed, changing tactics. "This is a different place than where we met previously."

"Wilder." The Ronin surveyed the periphery. "Wonder if our guest will be joining us."

"The Hunter." Questions bombarded Mavrik's mind as he tried to make sense of the situation. He took a stab in the dark. "The name, Errai, or the Shepherd King constellation mean anything to you?"

"Nope."

Of course not. He should have known better than to hope for convenience. Frustrated, he tossed out another question without thinking.

"What about, Eldorado?"

That stopped the Ronin. "Rings a bell." His jaw tightened, lips squirming, as though trying to force a memory from his mouth. The Ronin shook his head, conveying layers of disappointment. "Spent most of my life chasing after a treasure that couldn't be found."

*Your life?* Mavrik left this untouched, not ready to dive into those waters. A pomp didn't have a life, per say, because they didn't *live* as a human did. They were a cohesive assembly of psychological energy floating in the ether, shaped into a useable tool by a witch. Kept intact within the solidity of a numanen.

The Ronin said no more, ending the conversation. The pair lost themselves in the monotony of walking, engrossed in their own private ruminations.

The landscape changed, transitioning from plains to desert, the scraggly grass giving way to copper coloured sand and prickly plants that the Ronin called cactus. Blowing wind kicked loose detritus from dunes, creating twisting forms that danced across the sand. Strange rock columns the Ronin identified as hoodoos stood like sentinels, their forms disproportionally eroded. Mavrik caught an eerie sensation when gazing at the hoodoos that stood on either side of their route, but if the gunfighter felt a similar unease, he kept it to himself. Their shadows stretched far ahead as they entered this forest of rock sculptures.

Mavrik got the impression of being watched, his eyes darting amongst the empty spaces between individual hoodoos. A loud metallic clap sounded behind them and the sand at his feet erupted like a geyser. Another clap and something whizzed a handbreadth overhead. Mavrik spun about to see a group of five men emerging from a cloud of smoke. They carried rifles with bayonets attached.

There was a sizzle of flame, the Ronin shouldering him to the ground, then a puff of smoke activating a snaplock rifle. A hoodoo cracked, a line of fissures made by bullet impact. The Ronin lifted him up, shoving him off the trail and into the stone maze.

"La sorcière!" shouted the men, in pursuit.

Mavrik ran, blood pounding in his ears as he weaved

around the columns. He smelled gunpowder. Heard the others shouting in a language he didn't understand. He didn't know where he was going, didn't have a plan, was defenseless—

The Ronin grabbed him by the shoulder, pulling him behind a column with a squat base. He held a finger to lips for silence. The familiar handed over a revolver, handle first. Mavrik's first instinct was to protest, inwardly appalled by this transaction, mystified by its possibility.

*Stay here*, said the Ronin's hand gesture. *I'll double back.* Mavrik nodded his understanding, palm sweaty against the grip. The gunfighter departed in a crouch, stealthy as a prowling cat. Mavrik, back pressed to the stone, tried to calm his thunderous breathing.

Six bullets. Six opportunities to defend his Self. He'd never used any firearm before.

A bang and a scream. The Ronin was putting his other revolver to use. A flurry of rifle shots cracked against stone, raising a fresh cloud of smoke. The Ronin returned fire; he could reload. Strange echoes bounced off the hoodoos, making it seem as if the fighting was all around. Nearby, came the slow grind of a boot heel on loose gravel. Mavrik tensed, finger on the trigger.

A dark shape slunk into view and Mavrik's arm straightened, popping off two shots. One missed entirely, the other catching someone in the shoulder. A groan of pain changed into a battle roar. An attacker rushed Mavrik's position, bayonet at the ready. Mavrik squeezed the trigger. The man fell dead. Three shots remaining.

The clothing appeared to be handmade and the boots polished leather. A carefully trimmed goatee and a ruffled shirt. The rifle was a heavy and clunky thing embellished by ornate metalwork. Didn't seem like another former adversary of the Ronin.

An inhaled breath at his right ear instantly alerted Mavrik. He slammed his stomach to the ground; the rifle blast exploding above him. He stretched up and shot twice, dropping another man.

He rolled out of the smoke with one shot remaining.

Dead men on either side of his hiding spot. Not good. Mavrik moved on, hands steady despite his rapidly beating heart. Further off, it sounded like the Ronin was caught in a firefight. Mavrik chose a route with the intention of flanking the enemy while they were focused on the Ronin.

"Mourir sorcière!"

An attacker rushed forward, bayonet seeking to skewer Mavrik. He twisted and aimed, the rifle barrel cracking against his wrist and knocking the revolver away. Mavrik hopped backward, dodging the plunging blade of the bayonet. Eyes on the weapon, his heels landed on a decline and he slipped, dropping to his backside. The attacker advanced confidently, eyes blazing with zealous fire.

A shadow slithered between the columns, darkening beneath the other's leather boots. A vision of flowing white appeared. Graceful arms wrapped around the attacker's neck, twisting violently. Danya released her hold and the man flopped to the ground.

"Friends of yours?" asked Mavrik, reclaiming the revolver.

"Hardly," she said. "They threatened to burn me at the stake, so I poisoned them."

The Ronin's revolver let loose four shots in succession, leaving only the hiss of the wind against stone. The gunfighter approached, nodding to acknowledge a job done. Mavrik handed back the weapon, which the Ronin accepted with a lopsided grin.

A serviteur stood between two familiars, an action

supposedly impossible on multiple levels. Mavrik took a moment, trying to reconcile this arrangement, and failing.

"Look," said Danya, pointing to the hoodoos.

The stone flowed like water within the individual columns, swirling intensely. A column burst, its fluid melding into one adjacent. More stones detonated, latching onto and enlarging the first joining. Mavrik ran, his familiars following in unspoken agreement.

Explosions came all around them as the group raced along the path, intent on getting clear before the stone forest became a single object. He passed the threshold and kept going until the noise behind faded. Panting, he craned his neck skyward, marvelling at a towering mesa created by fusion. The flat top scraped a gold-flake cloud.

"Such chaotic power," Danya said musingly.

"Yep," said the Ronin.

Mavrik walked away, rattled by the fact that two psychopomps, supposedly under his control, were conversing without his involvement. The absence of kallikrates was like a hole inside of his Self, an emptiness as large as the unchanging sun still astride the horizon. The only constant in this strange land.

A lack of thirst or hunger accentuated Mavrik's nebulous grasp on time. The sun didn't move, the sky remained a golden haze, and the landscape was capable of drastic change irrespective of anything he knew regarding Anima or geography. Minimal commentary from the pomps had Mavrik wondering if they were as confused as him. They all paused while cresting a tall dune, surprised by a vivid change in colour; the desert abruptly transitioning to lush forest for no discernible reason.

The atmosphere amongst the trees was vastly different than the jungle on Kalubon, although Mavrik did find a sense of comfort in the familiar shade of a canopy. Soft ferns grew beside prickly hedges, interspersed by pale, smooth-barked trees. Occasionally there'd be a huge tree with rough, armour-like bark and twisting branches. Mavrik relished this first instance of encountering active, growing life in this world; breathing deeply for what felt like an age. His peacefulness turned out to be short-lived.

Horrifying howls careened from the forest depths. A pack of beasts craving blood. The howling changed frequency—shrieking, ecstatic and almost human as the beasts drew nearer. Mavrik and the two pomps turned towards the frenzy, peering at the undergrowth, into the terrible unknown of fate.

"You two get moving," said the Ronin, guns in hand. "I'll hold 'em off."

The shrieking wave was nearly upon them; the ferns were visibly shaking. Danya took Mavrik's arm, urging him away. He took a last glance at the Ronin: arms slack, barrels pointed at the earth. Mavrik and the Naga ran, but they couldn't outpace the skin crawling vehemence of the advancing din. Revolver blasts broke the unnerving cadence. Twelve shots, all chambers emptied.

Mavrik looked over his shoulder to see the Ronin hurrying after them, his expression tense, barely restrained from full blown panic.

"Go!" he bellowed.

The shrieking started again. Mavrik watched nine females rise, their hair wild, skin smeared with blood. Their mouths opening in fierce, mad grins, letting loose the bone-quivering screams.

"You were supposed to kill them!" Danya snapped, as the Ronin caught up.

"Didn't want to stay dead."

They sprinted headlong through the forest, heedless to tugs at their clothing and scratches to their skin. Stay ahead, stay clear. Only that mattered. But the women were gaining.

A black arrow smacked into a tree, vibrating with force. More arrows zipped overhead and crashed into the ground at their ankles. Danya hissed in anger.

"Keep running!" Mavrik urged.

He doubted her success in putting the madwomen down when the Ronin had failed. He also knew that if enraged she might stop and fight them anyway. White-hot pain flared in his calf muscle. Mavrik went skidding face first into the turf. The shaft of an arrow jutted out of his leg.

*That's it. I'm done for.*

Then, miraculously, he was back on his feet, the Ronin and Danya carrying him into a clearing. An oblong altar dominated the center; grapes and instruments and a human form on its surface. The familiars brought him around to the backside of the altar and set him down. They turned to make a last stand.

The shrieks were now cheers of victory.

The women raced into the clearing; crazed, dilated pupils locked onto the altar. They suddenly slowed and went quiet, advancing in a hesitant crouch. Bows and quivers were carefully set at the base of the altar, the psychopomps and witch ignored.

Each woman plucked a grape and ate with solemnity. One by one they began to hum, weaving together a beautiful harmony. With measured steps, they aligned into a crescent shape facing the altar. Their hair, matted and unruly, became clean and lustrous. Their skin, smeared and crusted in blood, became smooth and pure. Lastly, their eyes, wide and terrible, became bright and loving. The women gently clasped hands and faded into the light pouring forth from their eyes. There came the fluttering of wings and they were gone.

Mavrik, wincing, grabbed the top of the altar and pulled himself upright. He shook his head in disbelief at the figure laying on the stone—the Satyr, peaceful, and very dead.

Chikere's skin held a subtle greyness, his lower half covered by a pale blue robe. His mouth curved in a contented close-lipped smile.

"I don't understand," said Mavrik.

The Ronin put new shells into the revolvers while Danya examined the crescent where the women had stood. A ragged gasp tore out of Chikere, startling Mavrik. Chikere sat upright, using his knuckles to rub his eyes as he yawned.

"You're alive," said Mavrik, too shocked to be excited.

"Reborn, for all intents and purposes," said the Satyr. "Only my death could satisfy the priestesses."

Mavrik leaned against the stone for support, needing it in more ways than one. "But how?"

"Hemlock," said Chikere, matter-of-factly. "I put just the right amount in my wine to mimic death." He noticed the bows and arrows leaning against the foot of the altar. "A most convincing ruse!"

"Why did they want you dead?"

Chikere leapt down, ignoring the question. He poured a glass of wine, toasting to his own ingenuity. Mavrik hopped closer, stumbling, falling. Jolting pain obscured his need for questioning. Danya crouched beside him, her fingers on his injured calf.

"Be still," she said.

She pulled the arrow free in one smooth motion and all Mavrik could do was squeak. A soft, lilting song matched the caress of her fingers on his skin as she healed the wound. Moments later his leg felt as good as new.

"And for this they wanted to burn me," she scoffed, moving away.

Chikere's booming laugh carried throughout the clearing as he spoke with the Ronin. His skin was already returning to its usual robustness. The Ronin held his own cup, clinking it against Chikere's as he chuckled. Danya poked at the grapes, holding one aloft and inspecting it like a jeweller with a rare find. Mavrik's mind blanked, stupefied yet again. He moved closer, as if connected by gravity. As one, they turned to him.

"Where to?" asked the Ronin.

"What?"

"Our destination!" said Chikere.

"I…I don't know."

"Listen," said Danya, shushing the others. "What does your inner voice say?"

Mavrik listened, hearing nothing but the wind in the leaves and the rattling of his own doubts. Then, an indefinable something.

But no. Too faint, too fleeting.

There it came again, the softest of whispers pointing him in a direction.

"This way," he said.

Chikere chugged his wine, the excess dribbling down his chin. "Ah, to shake off the boredom of being dead." He finished by crushing the cup between his hands in a thunderous clap. "I live!"

"Lead on, Tasunka," said the Ronin.

"Is this your name?" asked Chikere, bushy eyebrows furrowed.

Mavrik shrugged. "One of them."

"What does it mean?"

"Horse," said the Ronin.

Chikere's confusion brightened into humour and Danya covered a smile. Mavrik started walking.

* * *

The forest floor began to pitch steeper, turning rockier as well. Tree height gradually declined in correlation to the slope until ceasing entirely as they reached an invisible vertical milestone. Craggy mountains framed the pass in which they traveled; landmarks that should have been visible from miles away. Mavrik didn't even bother questioning this bizarre change in terrain, although the sight of the sun, still peaking from a distance, did cause annoyance. Chikere sang, listening to his echo rebound off the mountainsides.

"Stop," said Danya, waving at the Satyr.

"You fear falling under my spell," said Chikere. "Many a woman has been entranced by my songs."

"There is something else, something worth hearing," she said.

"Nonsense! I—"

"I hear it too," said the Ronin.

Chikere quieted. Mavrik turned a slow circle, ears straining. A dull roar, like far off rolling thunder. But was it departing or approaching? They were near the peak of the mountain pass; small figures in a lonely space. Mavrik couldn't discern the origin of the noise, but he had decided that it was definitely coming closer.

"There," said the Ronin pointing to the mountain on their right.

"And there," said Danya, pointing to the mountain on their left.

Mavrik squinted, able to make out a swarm of black-clad figures running down the slopes. They were chanting and carrying flags. The two groups sharing a common mantra. He perceived an unmistakeable rage in their tone.

"They're going to cut off our route," said Mavrik, his gaze tracing the mobs' descent.

Chikere took off, arms pumping. "Forward!"

The others chased after the Satyr, their progress slowed by the incline. Mavrik spotted details within the mob: black hoods around faces covered by bandanas or gas masks, some holding signs and flags, others holding clubs. All were shouting in this furious, descending storm.

A glass bottle shattered ahead, exploding into a pillar of flame. Mavrik's group split, weaving around the acrid fumes. Metal canisters bounced off the rock, spouting streams of smoke as they tumbled. Mavrik hacked and coughed with tears stinging his eyes. The chanting mob was all around him. He pushed on blindly through the smoke.

Gouts of fire on the left, another spurting geyser ahead on the right. Mavrik ducked reflexively as an object whizzed overhead.

"EAT THE RICH!" bellowed the crowd.

Mavrik felt the ground flatten out; he'd reached the summit. The vibration from thousands of feet pounding toward his location coursed into his bones. Dark forms shifted in the grey on the periphery.

"Shit," said Mavrik.

Then the mob was upon him.

He dodged a swinging club, flinching at the proximity of a gun blast. His attacker fell backward as the Ronin spurred Mavrik onward. Danya screamed in rage; he glanced over to see a serpentine tail lash out from beneath her dress and strike a pair of assailants. Chikere's laughter, jubilant and frightening, cut through the chanting. The Ronin shot on the run, dropping hooded individuals in the smoke.

There were so many and he could feel their hatred

directed at him. Not at him personally, but what he represented. Their hostility and resentment striking a vein similar to his own opinion of Leadership.

The Ronin wheeled about, firing in a constant stream, just barely keeping them outside of the mob's clutches. Sparks leapt from his eyes, his face grim as a death mask. A disorganized wedge emerged out of the gloom, marching on Mavrik and the Ronin, leaving nowhere to turn. Mavrik picked up a fallen club and readied himself for the inevitable.

Bodies at rear of the mass went spinning through the air. People shouting in alarm as they were run-over from behind. The Satyr rammed his way through, punching a gap with his horns. The Ronin picked off the fringes. Mavrik knocked aside two at the vanguard and they charged into the opening. The Naga slithered up, protecting their flank with swift strikes.

Chaos raged around them as they floated in the eye of the storm. No time for thought or hesitation, only anticipation and death. Then they were clear of the smoke, beyond the violence and madness.

A solitary figure stood before them. As one, the familiars attacked, their features barely human.

"Stop!" Mavrik's command snapped like a whip. The pomps halted and withdrew: horns receding, tail shortening, blazing eyes fading.

The lone man crouched against a boulder, arms covering his face as he trembled.

"Zidati," said Mavrik. "From now on you fight your own battles."

The Politician uncurled, straightening his disheveled suit, still leaning against the rock. His mouth quivered, his face hardening to make a rebuttal, but he must have sensed that Mavrik wasn't to be tested at this moment, as he simply nodded.

The explosions and tear gas transformed into fireworks, the chanting into exultation. Joy sounded on the mountaintop, flowing into a collective catharsis. The vibration expanded, swiftly acquiring a directional current. Frothing white water crested the pass to overflow as a mighty river.

No time to run, no safe place. A wall of water slammed into Mavrik and the familiars, carrying them downstream.

* * *

Battered and bruised, Mavrik lay on soggy ground. He could still feel the rushing current around him: jostling, lifting, dunking. Powerlessness.

In the quiet, the disparate aspects of his Self rejoined, stitching him back together.

No sign of the others or where they had washed up. Vines drooped from mossy branches, the trees partially submerged in marshland. Mavrik must have collided with a rare patch of solid ground. Red light from the unrisen sun had difficulty penetrating the swamp, permitting pockets of darkness beneath the always golden sky. Finally, an area at least passingly similar to the Kalubon jungle, but the familiarity wasn't enough to improve Mavrik's mood.

Alone and directionless, he followed a strip of dry land weaving through the swamp. A dull ache twinging in his chest, more than physical, at the loss of the psychopomps. Their absence made clear an unnoticed connection, shocking Mavrik with its intensity. As a witch, he understood the connection to one's familiars through the numanens—a physical buffer. Now, he felt as if raw wounds were opening. Vulnerability was a disconcerting sensation for a serviteur, almost alien in its ability to warp his perception.

"Sweet love," came a woman's voice, liltingly. "Come to me, my sweet love."

Her pleasantness was wrapped around an iron core of command. A lingering reverberation of bitterness trembled the murky water. Mavrik turned to the voice, glimpsing a figure in crimson gliding between the trees, then fading into shadow. Not one of his.

"Sweetness," said the woman, calling out to him. Closer now. The hint of a growl in her tone.

Mavrik quickened his pace, foot sloshing into water with a misstep. Mud sucked at his heel, trying to claim the rest of him. He tugged his leg free, catching a blur of crimson creeping closer. Mavrik focused on the path ahead, trying to keep his distance from this newest pursuer, hoping that his familiars would come to the rescue.

"My love," she said, her irritation plain. "You did a bad thing. It hurts. My love!"

Mavrik ran; her voice right behind him. A heavy sigh in his ear as he felt her breath on the nape of his neck. He stopped, turning to face his fate.

No woman, just the dead calm of the swamp. From the corner of his eye he saw a crimson form slowly descending from the trees. An inhuman quality in the act made his flesh crawl.

"Lover," she said, her face shadowed in the depths of her hood. She crouched, one hand on the ground, the other elevated, fingers curled around a glittering thread. "My murderer."

He got the sense of more limbs tensing beneath her cloak. She tilted her head, exposing a flash of dark, shining eyes.

"Did you think this disguise could fool me?" The spider-woman released the thread, bringing her hands together as she crouched.

"I'm not—"

Her fingers flexed in his direction; gossamer threads gracefully sailing the separating distance. There came a sharp tug at his ankles. She closed one hand into a fist, cinching the threads tight. Mavrik's feet dropped out from under him and he slammed into the ground. She laughed softly, cruelly, and started reeling him in.

Mavrik dug his fingers into the dirt, clawing to stay free. A desperate hand hit a protruding object, half buried and indistinguishable from the soil. He gripped on, stalling his slide. She pulled harder but he wouldn't budge.

"Always so difficult," she mumbled.

His legs twisted, elevating as she ascended into the trees. A forceful wrenching lifted him vertical, his face at ground level. He lost his grip. The web pulling him higher.

Mavrik dug madly, trying to find the buried object amid the dirt and leaves. He saw it: what looked like a human hand sticking out of the ground, all knuckles and bone wrapped in leathery skin. Mavrik latched onto the hand, clasping as if in greeting. The skeletal hand squeezed back.

The spider-woman sang to herself, jerking him higher, his arms now fully extended. She pulled harder, her song altering in exertion. Mavrik and the skeletal hand clung to each other. Her singing paused as she reefed on the threads, bringing her prey that much closer. Mavrik gasped as the hand attached to an arm, connected to man, was lifted free of the earth. He recognized the tall black hat adorned with a peacock feather.

"Hello, madam," said Domagoj, the Sleeper. He didn't bow.

A sickle appeared in the hand that had gripped Mavrik. The weapon whistled into the heights, eliciting a brief shriek. The thread slackened and Mavrik crashed down.

"This is a crossroads," said Domagoj, turning in a slow circle as Mavrik disentangled his legs.

"Meaning?"

"Life and death have no claim here." The dark cavities of his eyes found Mavrik's. "A choice must be made."

"What kind of choice?"

Domagoj shrugged, continuing his examination of the environment. "We're being watched."

His senses told him nothing yet he sensed an approaching aura. Malevolence and despair, oily and heavy against his skin.

"The Hunter."

The beast roared, shaking leaves from the trees. Sparks and heat ripped throughout the swamp like ball lightning. The light expanded, bleaching away colour until everything became translucent. Mavrik blinked into blindness as the world disappeared.

* * *

Seconds, minutes, hours, days passed. All time or no time at all. Mavrik couldn't discern the duration, but the world returned with an unmistakeable sensation of *change.* The sun still straddled the horizon and yet now it had the feeling of being caught in a descent, unable to sink a final step and facilitate night. Blonde wisps of clouds grew into floating titans that shrank into nothing, only to repeat the process in a different area of the golden sky.

A solid line stretched across the landscape, straight and true amongst the rolling hills. A wall. Mavrik wondered what side of the barricade he was on.

Thrice his height and made of huge rectangular stone blocks, the wall asserted its dominance over Mavrik's vision, though, as he got nearer, he noticed crumbling sections and flaking mortar. This wall seemed heavily weathered and in need of repairs. A great iron door was set into the stone, its surface rusted to a shade like dried blood. Curious faces peeked over the battlements, followed by shouting.

There came a clink and creak of old chains straining: slowly, grudgingly, the gate lifted. It paused at eye level, this great hovering weight, for long enough that Mavrik thought the winch was broken. Then he realized they were waiting for him. A sharp inhale, his heart skipping a beat, and he ducked inside; clearing the gate with a few long strides. The chains wailed in their release, accompanied by a dense *whump* as the iron gate slammed into the ground.

"Tasunka, you made it," said the Ronin. The gunfighter looked more weary than relieved.

"Made it to where?"

"This is the first line of defense. The empire is under attack."

"What empire?"

The Ronin squinted. "I…I don't—"

Shouting from above stole his attention. "Shit."

He raced up a staircase carved into the back of the wall, taking two steps at a time.

Many other people milled about, in and out of several guardhouse structures, moving with purpose and urgency. All seemed to have a task. None had a face. A featureless grey blur, like a dirty mirror, obscured features and muffled voices. A person carrying quivers of arrows yelled something incoherent at Mavrik, forcing the witch to move aside. Mavrik shook his head in disbelief, following the Ronin's path, albeit at a slower pace.

Archers lined the walls around the gate while the gunfighter paced, his gaze focused on beyond the wall. A massive, jagged shadow appeared on the nearest hill. The shadow paused, its edges shifting and curling like smoke. Mavrik chuckled bitterly. The Hunter.

The shadow was on the move, causing the archers to reactively nock arrows to their bows.

The Ronin nodded to Mavrik. "Probably for the best if you go down below."

"I want to see this."

The Ronin turned to the enemy. "All right."

Sharp edges of the darkness concealing the Hunter jabbed like pincers as an acrid scent lifted in the air above the wall. Mavrik looked past this; the land behind the Hunter was now covered in shadow. A symphony of bowstrings released a storm of arrows.

Streaking points of death ricocheted off the midnight cloak. Menacing laughter rumbled out. The Ronin shot into the heart of the approaching darkness. The laughter stopped, shifting into a growl that set Mavrik's teeth on edge. Crackling bolts of blue electricity shot forth, lancing into many of the archers. Bodies dropped, their clothing singed, the air rank with burnt flesh.

Danya appeared on the battlement, tending to the fallen. The Ronin fired more shots at the hidden beast. Mavrik watched all of this in a state of detachment, his mind battling with his senses. Truth and belief locked in a stalemate.

Blue electricity struck the wall, ripping out chunks of stone. Dust particles mingled with the smoke, making the defenders fall into coughing fits. Drumming came from below, on the empire side of the barrier. Bleary-eyed, Mavrik watched Chikere march up the stairs banging a large, circular drum. The Satyr sang loudly, his voice resonating the particles within the smoke and clearing the air.

The remaining archers ditched their bows for drums, adding their own percussion to Chikere's. Danya continued to heal the wounded, adding more hands to the growing din. Mavrik felt the rumble trickling into the stone beneath his feet, working its way into the gaps of stone. Blue streaks crashed into the wall again and again. The vibratory rein-forcement held.

The shadow cover dissolved to reveal the Hunter's form: smoke covering its eyes, jaw clenched, hands balled into fists. The Hunter charged, bashing into the iron gate. Mavrik stumbled, but Chikere kept the song going.

Crash.

Crash.

They all felt the change in the impact as the iron began bending from the onslaught. Chikere's drumming trickled to a stop. His song couldn't touch the gate.

Zidati strode onto the wall, proudly facing their adver-sary. "We feel your anger, Wild One! We acknowledge your unrivalled strength!"

Anxious silence smothered the area in the momentary respite from the attack. Zidati, encouraged by this break, continued his plea.

"Let us make peace with one another. Let us chose diplo-macy instead of violence."

Silence. Zidati waited a beat or two, then inhaled to carry on with his oration.

"Let us come to an understanding through the sharing of words. May we—"

Crash.

Zidati wobbled, his confidence draining away. Iron bent unto breaking with a piercing screech. The Politician fled from his place on the wall.

Then, Domagoj was braced on the battlement with a long needle in hand. He stood directly above the gate, waving the needle, his eyes closed. Below came grunts of effort as the Hunter strove to enlarge the tear in the gate. Domagoj held the needle delicately, tip pointing down. With all eyes on the Sleeper, Mavrik went down the stairs.

The Hunter bashed and clawed at the ancient iron, hands

widening the breach. It sighted Mavrik's watching, jutting a pointing finger through the opening. Mavrik felt the animosity of the gesture in the pit of his stomach. The Hunter returned to its frenzied assault, mere moments away from gaining entrance. Mavrik waited, strangely numb.

Energetic lines descended into the gate from above, pulsing into the open space. These lines blocked the Hunter like bars in a jail cell. Atop the wall, Domagoj took off his hat and bowed.

The Hunter railed against the barricade, unable to burst through, it's growling frustration trailing into a whimper. Mavrik stepped closer, empathy attracting him to the obvious pain of the other. A hand on the shoulder spun him around. Mavrik grimaced, fist raised to strike.

"We did all we could do," said the Ronin. The other pomps were already leaving.

Mavrik looked back to the Hunter's raging, knowing that Domagoj's reinforcement wouldn't hold for long. He sighed, fist lowering, and went with the familiars, feeling pent up—unused.

They put the guardhouse at their backs, hurrying into the outlying hills, more intent on escape than destination.

A resonant boom stalled the group. The gate had fallen. Rather than dissipating, the sound intensified, ringing in Mavrik's ears. He clutched at his head, dropping to his knees. White light crowded his vision, merging with the vibration to negate all thought. He knew he was screaming. He knew it didn't matter.

* * *

Whispering all around him. Quiet shouting of contradicting opinions.

"Does he know?"

"How could he not?"

"I won't be the one to tell him!"

Hushed voices went silent as he opened his eyes.

"Tell me what?"

He lay in the shade of an apple tree, the branches mostly empty of fruit. Wrinkled, browning apples clustered the ground around him. The sun was directly above, at the peak of its transit. His familiars circled the tree, just outside of the cool ring of shade.

"The kingdom is coming apart," said Zidati, somberly.

Mavrik sat up, scratching his head. "I thought it was an empire?"

"The perimeter is breached," said Zidati. "Fracturing has begun. A concentration of resources is necessary for survival, thus the shrinking of dominion."

"The beast is inside," said Chikere.

"Hunting for you," said Domagoj, extending a boney finger.

"I already know that!" Mavrik snapped, coming to his feet. "Tell me something useful, like where we are."

"Eldorado," said the Ronin, eyes drifting up and around.

Mavrik recalled his first interaction with the Children of the Wolf outside of Imamu's cave. They'd claimed Eldorado to be an empire, a kingdom, a city, a king, a man. Apparently, the empire was already gone and the kingdom didn't have much time left. What was he supposed to do with that? Danya, noticing his frustration, brushed a hand on his shoulder.

"There are no answers to give," she said. "Only questions to be explored."

Errai. The Shepherd King. Eldorado. A crossroads. The Hunter. Mavrik tried to fit it all together. Failing to connect the pieces.

No numanens, yet here were his familiars. No kallikrates,

yet all manner of powerful transformations. Mavrik sighed, absently contemplating the rotting fruit at his feet. Almost imperceptibly, the emptiness inside of him grew. New territory added to the map of his Being in lines not drawn by his own hand.

"Onward," he said. "Wherever the path leads."

They came to a road of smooth black stone with raw knots of gold left unworked inside the hard substance. A pack of wild dogs fought over something in the ditch, snarling and snapping. The mongrels showed no fear of the approaching group, only scattering when the Ronin cracked a shot. Shredded clothing and dull red stains marked a pile of human bones.

Over the next rise they passed the smoking ruins of a farmstead, the structures crumbling into coal. Crops were razed and livestock slaughtered. Ravens squawked and croaked in a flurry of obsidian-shine feathers, squabbling over the carcasses. An uncaring sun watched from on high, beating down a relentless heat.

Variations of these scenes repeated in growing numbers as they traveled. The devastation was stark and recent. Out of the distant haze a growing mass gradually delineated into buildings of all sizes. A city of ghosts.


Gusts of wind stirred dust-devils in the empty street. Open doors slammed as the miniature cyclones passed.

"This is a dead place," said Chikere, nose tilted.

"So much pain," said Danya. "Sunk into the roots."

Domagoj wandered off to examine claw marks raked across a wall. Mavrik listened to the wind, entranced by a change in pitch. A woman's voice calling, indistinct yet familiar. He forgot about the others, following the voice into what seemed to be the city square.

A fountain in the center spouted dirty water, flowing into a muddy basin. Weeds jutted from cracks between cobblestones leading to a stately building. Grand domes seemed out of place, perched as they were on faded walls overgrown with vines. The climbing plants were everywhere, as if trying to strangle the building into submission. Crumbling steps flattened into a gaping entryway; the interior a matte black. The voice poured out of this secretive opening, drifting down the stairs, imploring Mavrik to continue.

A distinct feeling of comfort flowed within the voice, tugging at the emptiness inside of Mavrik, circling the space and growing louder. He had to go, had to know. Determined, in a drifting sort of way, he started for the steps; a firm hand on his shoulder stalling him.

"Careful," said Zidati. "Things that seem too good to be true usually are."

"You hear it?"

Zidati ran a hand over his bald head. "I hear something. Too faint to trust the source."

The Ronin approached, an uncharacteristically vacant look in his eyes.

"A voice?" asked Mavrik.

The Ronin blinked, nodding slowly, his gaze shifting to suspicion while regarding the abyss atop the stairs. The other three familiars entered the square, all drawn to the sound emanating from here.

"Seems like the choice is made," said Mavrik, starting up the stairs.

Zidati sighed wearily, following closely with the others a few steps behind.

A scent of slow rot crowded the darkness, a mustiness of mold eating away at the structure. Sunlight slanted through a few windows high up, a tint in the glass making a crisscross of pale red beams. Flames lifted into existence with

Mavrik's first step past the threshold; delicate bits of fire twisting on tall, white candles. Candlelight displayed a series of corridors and stairways, while keeping their destinations hidden. Mavrik noted an accumulation of mushrooms growing out of the walls, their bulbous heads covered in condensation.

The voice became fuller, more textured and alive.

"Who calls us?" asked Mavrik.

Pale figures appeared deeper within the interior, their forms shifting between solid and transparent. The voice divided amongst these forms, transitioning into various tones. Mavrik felt a pulling at his attention towards the nearest staircase. The pomps seemed drawn in directions of their own. Without deliberation, the group split, each following an intoxicating invitation.

A woman waited for Mavrik at the next landing, drifting away as he climbed.

"Wait," he croaked, gripped by a sudden desperation.

"Hurry," said the woman.

Mavrik tripped over the final stair to see her ethereal form glide through a closed door. Heart pounding, he gripped a doorknob shaped like a blooming rose. Caution poked at his awareness, but its intensity was swiftly cooled by the beseeching voice on the other side of the doorway. Body tingling in anticipation, he entered.

Lamplight illumined a neatly made bed. Roseline sat on the edge facing him.

"You found me!" She smiled, eyes sparkling with happiness.

Mavrik frowned; he was angry with her about something important. But what?

"Come," she said, rising.

He obeyed, carried over in a trance. She pressed her body close.

"Lover," she gasped, kissing his neck. "I'm yours." She bit his earlobe.

Firm, caressing hands urged him onto the bed. Electricity trickled across his skin, dampening the concern in his mind. Hungry fingers clawed at his clothing as his own found the curve of her hips. His body was fire, desirous and ready to give her whatever she wanted. Yet, inside, the emptiness in his chest expanded.

"What have you brought for me?" she purred.

"What?"

"Gold, have you brought any gold?"

Caution, only silenced and never cowed, came screaming back. He pushed away from her, shocked by the malice in her eyes, her appetite appearing more than carnal. Mavrik scrambled to his feet, retreating from her vicious grin.

"I know you have it," she said, coyly. Her form flickered, her face bloody and ravaged, then once again smiling and beautiful. "Jackal," she spat the name like a curse. "Coward!"

Mavrik back-pedalled out of the room, losing his balance while turning in the hallway and falling through an open doorway.

There came a fluttering of wings above, concealed by darkness. Soft electric string-lights conveyed a rounded room. Imamu sat on a rug, unimpressed with his awkward entrance.

"About time you showed up," she said.

Mavrik moved toward his teacher, heart filling with concern for her safety. Safe from what? She motioned for him to sit and he obliged.

"My student," she said, appraisingly.

The tone of disappointment stung his pride.

"Did I not care for you?" she asked.

Mavrik nodded.

"Did I not help you to survive?"

A smaller nod, stuck on the lump in his throat.

"Then why do you withhold from me?"

Her accusation put him on the verge of weeping. He would do anything to make things right with his teacher. He met her gaze, her hardness softening, her gaze hopeful.

"Have you brought any gold?"

"Gold?"

"Whatever you have," she said, comfortingly. "Place it at my feet."

The overhead wingbeats circled lower, just out of sight. Mavrik stared at Imamu in confusion. She flickered, face ashen and clothing soaked in dark red stains.

"This is wrong," he said, moving to his feet.

Cawing ravens landed around her, their dark eyes matching her own.

"I know you have it," she said.

He backed away, skin crawling with unease.

"Two Handed Hoarder," said Imamu. She snorted in disgust. "Thief!"

He was back in the hallway. No sign of the stairs. Only a waiting door, that of his childhood home. Mavrik pressed a finger to the lock and stepped inside.

He inhaled sharply, heart skipping a beat, stunned at the sight of his mother.

"Don't just stand there," she said, smiling. "Come, give me a hug."

Mavrik rushed over and embraced her. He didn't want to let go. Why had he ever let go in the first place?

"My boy," she said. "I'm so proud of you."

Joy emblazoned inside, thrilling him with its purity. He felt as though he could do anything, empowered by her blessing. And yet...the emptiness in his chest steadily ate away at his joy, gnawing it down to nothing.

She gripped him lightly by the biceps, looking up with concern. "What's wrong, my son?"

"I don't know."

She placed a palm on his chest. "A heavy burden. One you no longer need to carry alone."

"Yes." He wished so badly to be free of it.

"Share this with me."

A tear trickled down his cheek. Her compassion thrumming through his veins. "Thank you."

"Hurry now," she said. "We haven't much time."

"How do I…what do I…"

"Just a little bit of gold," she said, sweetly. "Share with me. Be free of your burden."

Pain lanced into his ribcage. She flickered, her touch going cold and clammy. He pulled away.

"You died," he said.

"Silly boy, I'm right here."

"No." He retreated.

Her loving expression twisted into a scowl. "Sixfold," she said, contemptuously. "Murderer."

A violent crash below shook the building. A bellow of rage echoing in the halls. Mavrik ran for the stairs as another impact rocked the structure, debris falling around him as walls toppled.

He raced for the main entrance, ducking as shards of glass rained down. Chikere bolted out of the building. Then Zidati and Domagoj. He spun, looking for the others.

"Move, you fool!" Danya hissed as she sidestepped him.

The Ronin, where was the gunfighter? He spotted the familiar across the way, stock-still as though entranced.

"Ronin!"

No response.

Crackling bolts of blue energy shattered a staircase. The

Hunter was inside. Mavrik ran for the Ronin, slipping on the slickness of mushrooms underfoot.

He grabbed the other by the shoulders. "Come on!"

The Ronin's weary eyes looked up from beneath the wide brim of his hat. "I think I'll stay, Tasunka."

"This place is about to fall on our heads!"

The Ronin looked around at the destruction and nodded. "She's going to tell me my name."

A huge section of the domed ceiling smashed into the floor.

"I need to know," said the Ronin.

A ghostly feminine form materialized, taking the gunfighter by the hand and leading him away. Mavrik ground his teeth in frustration and made for the exit; the Hunter appearing on the far side of the dome wreckage, shadows swirling as he gazed squarely at Mavrik.

"It's all your fault," said the Hunter, deep and grating.

Mavrik stumbled out of the opening and down the stairs, turning back to see the final collapse. He dropped to his knees.

"He stayed," Mavrik said in disbelief. A pomp shouldn't be able make a refusal.

Tentacles of the Hunter's power sifted through the ruins from below.

"We should go," said Zidati, helping Mavrik to his feet.


The city transformed as they walked, the buildings melting to be reshaped as wet clay in an unseen potter's hands. Mavrik hardly noticed; the Hunter's accusation imparting guilt for the loss of the Ronin. A voluminous haze of clouds obscured the sun, dropping the temperature and dimming the light.

The refashioned city made no sense: houses with thatched roofs squatting next to metal skyscrapers, narrow brick three-stories beside colossal stone monuments, adobe huts adjacent to timber-frame. Some structures burned, their snapping flames not traveling next door to the neighbour. Others teetered on the verge of collapse, while others had more broken windows than not. None seemed lived in.

Danya gasped in alarm, hurrying over to a cottage with a stone chimney surrounded by herbs and wildflowers. "This is my house!"

It took several moments for Mavrik to comprehend what she'd said. Realization did not help him formulate a question that sounded sane.

"Quaint," said Zidati, observing from a distance.

"It was taken from me," said Danya. "I remember now! I had to flee." She bent amongst the flowers, breathing deeply and smiling. "This was my oasis, my sanctuary."

"And now it has returned to you," said Chikere. "Good fortune!"

Danya straightened, staring at the purple door. "I never want to leave again."

"You approach a threshold," Domagoj warned.

"Wait a second," said Mavrik, too late. Danya was already nearing the door.

She glanced over her shoulder before ducking inside and closing the door behind her. The cottage vibrated, energetic lines wavering on its surface and expanding into its depth. There came a solid *whoosh* as the building vanished. Mavrik gaped at the patch of hard-packed dirt.

"She's gone," he said.

Chikere swung his head this way and that as he turned in a circle. "Do you feel that?"

Mavrik shook his head, to Chikere's disappointment.

"A rumble like the grind of the earth," said the Satyr. "It resonates in the marrow of my bones." He snapped to attention. "This way."

The others struggled to match Chikere's long, effortless stride. They caught up to him in front of a round structure of stone blocks ringed by columns supporting a tiled roof. Chikere was crying uncontrollably.

"What is this place?" asked Mavrik, knowing it couldn't be a home.

Chikere dried his eyes and wiped the snot from his nose. "My family tomb." He sighed and looked to the sky. "I spurned the obligation of being interred here. All of my blood kin are inside."

Mavrik spotted the look of resignation, his pulse quickening. "You don't have to go inside. You're strong and healthy."

Chikere chuckled, a little sad. He clapped a hand on Mavrik's shoulder. "I died alone and unremembered long ago in a forest far away."

He started toward the tomb. "I have returned! Did you miss me?"

Chikere rolled aside the stone slab and squeezed inside. He winked at the others then rolled it closed. Undulating lines of energy hummed throughout the structure until *whoosh*. Mavrik slowly shook his head. He looked blankly at Zidati and Domagoj.

"Are you planning on leaving too?"

"Unlikely," said Zidati, somewhat annoyed.

"Homes and burials never held much sway with me," said Domagoj.

"All right." Mavrik rubbed his face roughly. "Let's keep going."

They passed buildings of all shapes, sizes, and materials from different eras. Mavrik silently fumed, unseeing to all of it, until an appearance of familiar tech caught his eye. It wasn't much more than a shack, but it could have been plucked out of Siridea. Intrigued, he approached, the door sliding open automatically.

A single bed, a simple washroom, and a small seating area, but the walls are what grabbed his attention. Markings were carved into every surface; sets of four lines with a fifth crossed over their width.

"Like a prison cell," said Zidati.

Mavrik found where the counting stopped: two vertical lines.

"Three days left," said Domagoj. "There's no other space remaining."

Disorientation occluded Mavrik's vision; he was seeing double, as though in two separate locations simultaneously. Hands that were not his own extended from his body to latch onto a mechanical orb resting on a narrow pedestal. Lines of energy entered into the orb from north, south, east, and west. Agonizing pain wracked his nervous system. Anima from his Being was forcefully implanted into the orb as the lines reconfigured into a twelve-sided dodecahedron.

He couldn't take anymore. Mavrik ripped away from the world of this other, the connection held by a thread of bitter despair. The thread issued from his chest, from the nucleus of the growing emptiness. Existential terror throttled him as he tried to distance his Self. The thread stretched long, hair thin, until finally sinking into his chest.

He opened bloodshot eyes to see a crouching Domagoj watching in amusement. Mavrik lay on the floor of the Siridean shack.

"Where did you go?" asked the Sleeper.

"The worst place I know." Mavrik sat up, his body stiff, as though rigid for hours. "The markings are a countdown."

"To what?' asked Zidati, from the entrance.

"I don't know."

"Something evil," said Domagoj, with a knowing grin.

"Yeah, nothing good," Mavrik agreed.

He twitched at a sharp searing pain in his chest, like being pricked by burning thorns. Emotion flooded his awareness—too much to disseminate. He felt as if he was going to die there on the floor. No, worse, he knew he would *live* and this suffering would endure. The thorns dug deeper, slashing and searing. Mavrik screamed.

His existence was torment, agony his purpose. He was unable to break away, forced to endure, his freedom denied.

A small aspect of his Self withstood the onslaught; a shining golden core.

Light pulsed from this nucleus, combating the pain spreading from the emptiness. The forces intermingled until both were neutralized. Mavrik gasped in a lungful of air. Domagoj smacked him on the back and regular breathing resumed.

"Gentlemen," said Zidati in alarm. "Strange moving shadows and smoke are coming closer, and the occasional building is being destroyed."

"On your feet," said Domagoj, helping the witch up.

"He's still after us," said Mavrik. "Hunting me."

"Splendid motivation for moving forward."

"Closer!" Zidati was almost shrill.

They departed from the shack, running between buildings until forced to a halt. An immense castle blocked their escape. More precisely, a wide moat surrounding the castle blocked their escape. Bursts of explosions came from the area of the shack.

"What do we do?" asked Zidati.

"Swim," Domagoj replied. "Then climb."

Mavrik focused on the drawbridge; he'd been through too much for it to end here.

"I want to see what's next. I want to finish this."

The drawbridge groaned, released from its mooring and descending with frightening velocity to slam into place at their feet.

"Gentlemen," said Mavrik, ushering them inside.

He was past the point of questioning, fully navigating that murky terrain between survival and transcendence.

The sky suddenly changed so completely and powerfully that he staggered to a stop. The static golden background was now an irrepressible, slow flowing blue-black. Saffron clouds became a shimmering silver. A great shining moon replaced the sun—its dark scores of pits and craters displayed proudly. He paused for a moment to contemplate the meaning, but the drawbridge remained lowered and the Hunter drew near. He gave up on thinking and chased after the familiars.

He entered a courtyard filled with granite figures—what appeared to be a multitude of male sculptures in a variety of poses. Their colouration differed from white-flecked to pinks, browns, mottled greens and blue-greys, but they all seemed to be based on the same inspiration; one Mavrik Omolara.

The witch slowed, confusion and anger vying for control as he passed his own visage in every conceivable expression. A great surge of wind blew into the courtyard, violently crashing statues into each other and tipping them over. Mavrik dodged a falling replica, flinching at the stone debris. The wind howled, as joyful and destructive as a child at play. Statues crashed and shattered all around, forcing Mavrik to rush into the yawning opening of the castle proper.

Moonlight stretched across a tiled mosaic floor and hanging tapestries as the wind raged outside. The echoes of his steps faded into the immensity of the castle interior. He quickly outpaced the reach of the moon and was left to walk in darkness.

The castle took on the sense of an enormous cave, imparting a staleness of dormancy and the weight of being buried beneath countless tons of rock. Mavrik felt the emptiness in his chest resonate with this endless, crushing dark; quickening as if aware of the environment. Fear tickled across his skin, raising the hairs on his neck and forearms. Understanding, cold and clear as lake ice stopped him—this enlarging emptiness would not cease, it would claim his body entirely. Like the ominous countdown discovered in the Siridean shack, the serviteur was running short on time.

A powerful, sweet scent pulled him from his revelation. Burning incense drifted toward him, spiralling and strangely visible despite the lack of light. Like curled fingers the wisps enticed him onward. A flicker and crackle of flames splattered across the walls, soon illuminating the silhouettes of Domagoj and Zidati. Mavrik called to the pomps but the Sleeper and Politician paid him no mind. Mavrik came abreast, gasping at the scene of their focus.

An intricately wrought golden throne dominated the chamber. High backed and implacable, it seemed to flow with the movement of the flames set on torches on either side. A pair of giant shaggy dogs slumbered at the foot of the throne, their blocky heads resting on broad paws. Their coats were red-gold and so voluminous around the neck as to resemble a lion's mane. The beasts, obviously guarding this seat of power, breathed deeply as the trio of interlopers observed in silence. The incense appeared to be coming from the throne, lifting from the golden surface in thin tendrils, then coalescing into traveling spirals.

Mavrik looked to the others: Domagoj being unreadable and Zidati conveying a barely contained glee. Zidati appeared mesmerized at the prospect afforded by the throne, dangerously oblivious to the threat posed by the guard dogs.

"Finally," he whispered, "the reward for all of my service."

Domagoj cast a wary eye on the Politician. Mavrik motioned for silence.

"I *deserve* this," said Zidati, louder now.

Mavrik winced at the volume, sighing heavily as two shaggy heads lifted upright, brown eyes alert. Zidati's words rebounded throughout the chamber, sometimes thinner and sometimes denser. Domagoj watched the returning echoes as if they were a flock of startled birds.

"Use wisdom in every uttering," he said softly.

Zidati stepped into the chamber, causing the dogs to rise, their teeth bared while growling menacingly.

"Sit," said Zidati, with uncompromising command.

The dogs obeyed, moving to frame the throne. They watched Zidati approach as if undecided about ripping him to shreds or desiring further command. Zidati's hands lifted unconsciously, reaching for the throne in yearning.

"They kept this from me," he said bitterly. "Those self-righteous, riotous, ungrateful plebs." The throne pulsed, coming alive with his words. Zidati chuckled harshly. "Where are their votes now?"

The throne radiated an inner light, drawing Zidati forward like a magnet. He sat, satisfied. His enjoyment was short-lived; concern flashing across his eyes, his forehead creasing. He struggled, unable to raise his hands from the armrest. His head and neck stuck to the backrest, his legs locked in place. The dogs howled, their baleful cries reverberating throughout the chamber.

Throne-light filtered into every part of Zidati's body until only the outline of his form was distinguishable. He tried to speak, succeeding in spewing a cloud of incense. The light flared, all-consuming, then swiftly fading. The howling came to an end. The throne sat empty, placid and inviting.

"He got what he wanted, more or less," said Domagoj.

Mavrik stared at the watchful guardians, actively avoiding the golden seat. *What do I want?*

"Guidance. I need guidance."

His words thrummed through the chamber, intensifying the further they traveled. A figure stepped out of the dark behind the throne, casually resting a hand on one dog's head. Mavrik's jaw dropped, his shock giving way to joy.

"Mav," said Oberon. "You're grown." He scratched behind the dog's ear and stepped forward.

"Grandfather…"

"I'd always hoped we'd meet again, just didn't think it would be during your own Pilgrimage."

A jolt shuddered through Mavrik—of course, he was on Pilgrimage. He snorted at his own stupidity.

"This is as far I journeyed in my time," said Oberon. He smiled, bittersweet. "My brother and I fought for the throne. He claimed it."

"And lost his ability to speak kallikrates."

"I did what I could for Kalubon, but true healing was beyond my understanding." He looked to Mavrik, eyes bright and hopeful. "The best I could do was create a bridge for another to cross."

"My father was unworthy." Doubt shaded his words. *Am I worthy?*

"Ivaylo and I quarrelled about many things. Eldorado was our final disagreement."

"What should I do?"

"Do you want the throne?"

"No." The answer came quick and true. "I'm not ready and not sure if I'll ever be."

"Then move forward. There are two more stages."

Mavrik and Domagoj exchanged a look: two more stages plus this one makes three. Three ticks to go on the scratch-marked countdown.

"How?"

Oberon glanced at the foot of the throne. "Don't underestimate the power of a humble question."

Mavrik swallowed and Oberon stepped aside. He approached, tears in his eyes, and knelt before the throne, placing his hands on the cool stone.

"How do I proceed? Please, I ask for guidance."

Head bowed, forehead touching down, he asked from his heart, openly, vulnerable.

There came a wet snuffling at his ear. Mavrik was face-to-face with a giant dog. The other was already walking away into the dark.

Mavrik smiled. "Thank you."

He and the final pomp followed the dog. Oberon had vanished. As they walked after the guardians into the recesses of the chamber, Mavrik paused to look back at the distant spot of gold. Jagged bolts of blue wracked the throne, toppling the seat of power. The Hunter's hulking form claimed this new territory.

"There is a light ahead," said Domagoj.

Mavrik hurried to catch up, finding the dogs waiting at a portal shaped like a human eye. The region around the pupil glowed faintly and the pupil itself was a dark, pulsing space.

"Onward," said Mavrik.

"Inward," said Domagoj, stepping into the portal.

Mavrik followed the pomp's example while the Hunter's enraged roar echoed behind him.

* * *

All was dark. Blacker than a starless night.

Mavrik took a tentative step. The floor rippled like water. The emptiness inside of his chest became exultant, threading deeper and more thoroughly into his body. A body that he felt to be much smaller, that of a child. Mavrik was now a boyhood version of himself. Pain, recent as the loss of his mother, bubbled beneath the surface of his mind, steadily rising to an incapacitating boil.

"I see something," said Domagoj.

The Sleeper departed, the sound of his rippling footsteps becoming fainter. Panic swelled within Mavrik as he struggled to catch up. A glimmer of white light appeared, tall and narrow, and infused with silver flecks. A chair of smooth, curving design as ephemeral as a moonbeam, illuminating a small circle in this endless dark.

Mavrik noticed that Domagoj appeared more human than he'd ever been before. The Sleeper's smooth black skin and trim beard were now that of a handsome, middle-aged man. Domagoj's eyes misted over with unshed tears. He bowed his head, removing his hat, jacket, and leather shoes.

"What are you doing?" asked Mavrik.

"Saying thank you. I never hoped to have this chance."

"For what?"

"Absolution." Domagoj reluctantly pulled his focus away from the chair to lock eyes with Mavrik. "Long ago I made a deal I came to regret. I was granted great power for a great price. I was selfish, and proud, and blind to my own pain." He smiled, his previous skeletal grin a pale shadow to this serene expression. "Time has a way of humbling a person."

He nodded to Mavrik in acknowledgement and stepped toward the chair to climb hand over hand. In the seat now, the white light began to flutter like the flapping of thousands of wings. Energy swirled around the chair as it seemed to ascend and descend simultaneously. Mavrik blinked and his last familiar was gone.

Darkness returned, absolute in its authority. Mavrik felt intimately alone, terrifyingly so. His boyhood-ness claimed control over his mind.

"Mother," he said, in a ragged whisper. "I want my mother!"

The emptiness in his Self surged, racing through his blood, saturating his flesh. Mavrik screamed in agony, consumed by fear. He tried to resist the onslaught, his efforts futile. Bit by bit he was devoured. Mavrik fell, curling on the ground, wrapped around his grief. The emptiness had him.

Shame. Guilt. Self-loathing. Sour emotions roiled within him like entwining serpents. His small, frail physical form was at their mercy, and they were merciless. And then, he stopped fighting, instead choosing acceptance, abandoning the hopes of his previous reality.

There was no escape. No making things right.

The torment calmed, smoothening into a pliable substance. Mavrik realized he was no longer alone in the dark.

"My son," said Ivaylo.

His father stood over him, visible even as the world remained without light. Mavrik saw the sneer that he knew well from his childhood. A vibration trembled at the edge of Mavrik's awareness, the hint of sound at its core.

"Your weakness ruined everything," said Ivaylo. "If only you'd obeyed me, then we'd still be a family."

The vibration took on a feeling of form within Mavrik—round and solid as a gong. He observed it in his mind's eye, sensing its capacity to resonate.

"Your fear infected your mother, turning her against me," said Ivaylo. "I wanted to save everyone. I would have been a hero. The world could have achieved peace."

Mavrik saw it then, plain and unmistakeable: his father's fear. Even now it ate away at Ivaylo's insides. Ivaylo clamped down on it again and again, attempting to control and over-power. The strain of this constant silencing being reflected outward. Directed at him.

Sadness washed through Mavrik, coating the surface of the instrument floating in his mind's eye. An unstruck sound reverberated throughout him, beautifully painful, musical and boundless.

"I'm sorry," said Mavrik. "I'm sorry you didn't have the life you wanted."

Rage flared in Ivaylo's eyes, his jaw clenching. He looked ready to strike. Mavrik sat upright, so small beneath his father's towering despair. The resonance inside of Mavrik burst into particles of golden dust, drifting aimlessly.

"Fulfill my dream," Ivaylo commanded.

Crackling blue light rapidly approached, forcing Ivaylo to step back, his attention drawn to this approaching aura.

The Hunter leapt. A huge fist arced to destroy Ivaylo. Mavrik's father, calmly and swiftly lashed out with a devastating backhand, sending the Hunter to the ground.

The Hunter surged upright and Ivaylo latched a vice grip around its throat, tossing the menacing being back down. Mavrik stared, wide eyed, as the Hunter struggled to rise. Ivaylo kicked repeatedly, beating down this unstoppable menace.

"Stop," said Mavrik. "I don't understand."

"Still a child in so many ways," said Ivaylo. "You don't even know who, or what, this is."

The Hunter lay on the dark, watery surface, breathing shallowly. Ivaylo advanced, confident in his superiority.

"Your familiars," said Ivaylo, "they are not psychopomps. Even someone as dense as you has started to suspect this." He tilted his head, relishing his eminent knowledge. "They are you. You are them. Each one is a past Self, a different incarnation of the same spirit."

The gold dust inside of Mavrik gusted wildly, coming to life with unrecognized realization. His father only had one familiar. Mavrik's pain transformed into understanding. Ivaylo had been jealous of him. Resentful that his son could be the hero instead of his own Self. Cascading golden dust coalesced into spheres in Mavrik's heart and mind.

"I forgive you," he said.

The light within him pulsed and Ivaylo staggered.

"What did you say?"

"You are forgiven."

Mavrik moved to his feet, forcing Ivaylo backward. Able to see eye to eye with his father; he was no longer a boy. Ivaylo flinched. Mavrik grew brighter.

"No," said Ivaylo. "We can make a new arrangement."

Golden light emanated from Mavrik's form, causing Ivaylo to appear as a silhouette.

"Please," said his father, "don't do this to me."

"It was never about you," said Mavrik. "I see that now."

Ivaylo cowered, shrinking from the presence of his son. Mavrik leaned down, extending a hand, supporting the Hunter to its feet. Ivaylo dwindled into obscurity until completely released.

Mavrik recognized these hands—they were the same as those from his out of body experiences. The countdown was the Hunter's work. The Hunter was the one having his Anima repeatedly taken and placed into the orb.

"A numanen," said the Hunter, as if reading Mavrik's mind. "The orbs are energy-containers that Kalubon exports to the Alliance."

The drifting smoke around the Hunter faded and Mavrik saw the other clearly for the first time. A man, not a wicked psychopomp.

"I can't go on any longer," said the Hunter, "and they won't let me die."

"What is your name?"

The Hunter paused, his face a hard mask, and Mavrik thought the other might refuse to answer.

"Ekundayo." He shuddered. "More and more I am forgetting my Self."

"I understand why you have pursued me," said Mavrik, the goldenness inside beginning to solidify. "You are a future Self, seeking to put an end to your suffering. A suffering that my actions have generated."

"I couldn't die, but I thought if I killed you then maybe…" Ekundayo looked into the nothingness. "Then we arrived here and for the first time in my life I felt hope. I needed to push you to continue, to—"

"Transform."

Mavrik's body appeared as living gold; a stark contrast to Ekundayo's ashy complexion and ragged clothing, and yet, they were the same Being.

"I was never meant to be a hero," said Mavrik. "I am a healer."

Light exploded out of him, connecting with the light that had always been within the darkness, revealing understanding beyond words. He was all there, every form and incarnation. All of their experiences and realizations were his and all of his were theirs, because they were one. The string of time revealed itself to be connection.

Mavrik, his awareness centered on who he'd been and who he now was, moved seven pairs of hands in unison; the hands having been made clean and fresh as a newborn. Selfless at his most Self-full.

His hands were a bowl made to share love in the form of healing, able to plant seeds that might grow into what they would become, seeds to be planted in kindness.

"I am," the realization arising as a vibration marrying thought, feeling, and word.

He rested in an eternal-instant of unity, a peacefulness restoring his true Self. The embrace gradually dimmed, the light fading, and with it came a sense of his body. Mavrik knew that he needed to return. His work was unfinished.

The plane of Eldorado, recognizing his awareness, pushed him through the Shepherd King gate and back to Kalubon.

# PART III

# MATTER OF POSSIBILITY

Unity shifted from all-encompassing to all-constituting, becoming part of him rather than he being part of it.

Layers of reality compiled as they were enmeshed, creating a perception of distance between Mavrik's awareness and the goldenness of Eldorado. There was too much for him to hold within the physical boundaries of his mind—the speed, the brilliance, and the endlessness exceeding the capacity of his grasp. He let go, realizing there was no need to hold on to this power from a different plane. He smiled, understanding that access was a matter of openness. Breathing calmly, peacefully, he exchanged control for collaboration.

His human eyes opened in the familiar dimness of Imamu's cave. Fingers of sunlight poked around the cave mouth and the damp heat of Kalubon's jungle greeted him like an old friend. Mavrik noticed a coating of dust on his teacher's objects, the unchecked growth of seedlings as Nature reclaimed this space. Imamu was gone, but this degree of change to her residence should not have occurred so quickly.

Mavrik picked up his wooden mask that lay discarded nearby—unable to recall leaving it here. Perhaps Rouey brought it for safe keeping. Rouey. His friend had been writhing on the floor from a tase-jolt during Mavrik's abduction.

The chaos of the Dome's collapse amidst the ashfall came rushing back, as well as Ikenna's malicious subterfuge. A chilly premonition of Ekundayo's fate swept through Mavrik at the realization of its connection to Ikenna's Fortress. Mask in hand, he exited the cave, ready to make the long walk to Siridea.

The world seemed different, imbued with an ineffable and pervasive sadness. To Mavrik it felt most akin to the separation of mother and child; loss and fear and love all melding into an unresolved mix. He came to the terraced rice paddies and stopped, staring uncomprehendingly at the destruction.

Half of the human-made mountain was rubble, the orderly green a melee of jagged stone. The debris appeared well-settled, raising the hairs on Mavrik's neck. *How long have I been gone?* Time had not ceased during his Pilgrimage, this crucible of existence unbothered by his individual endeavour. He began to temper his expectations about the state of the city. His home. His friend.

He'd always assumed the environment, the city, and the people of Kalubon to be separate things that were related to one another yet essentially detached. Each a reservoir of Anima in its Self. This assumption suddenly seemed ridiculous. The power inherent *in relationships* became apparent as more fundamental than the *entities* on their own. A great pattern emerged in his awareness—layers upon layers supporting myriad aspects of being. Harmony through the communication of differences.

The various relations between entities enabled living organisms to develop and thrive. Power resided within the connections, constantly transferring between individuals on all levels, from the smallest and invisible to the most tactile and expansive.

Kalubon had shaped him, yet he had been a co-creator in this process. For most of his life he'd felt separated from the world, a distinct piece set aside from the rest, pushed and pulled by tensions too overarching and ingrained to be challenged, yet he had fought them all the same.

In this moment he was five past Selves and a future Self. In Siridea he was Jackal, Two Handed Hoarder, Sixfold and the Blood of Oberon. A serviteur. A witch. A student and a healer. He bowed his head, accepting the fate conveyed by his lineage as well as the responsibility of the choices he'd made along this path.

He felt an inner shift, a threshold reached; transmuting the thread of fate that for years had seemingly controlled his life into one of destiny. He was now an active participant within the energetic harmony.

The connections blazed in golden light, endlessly creative, intimately relational. Anima was not static, never had been. Anima lived, expressed through every interaction. Maverick gave thanks for this wisdom while realizing it did not change the task at hand. The whirring of surveillance drones lifting off from outlying structures were a clear reminder of the adverse forces who wanted him to fail. Several of the insectoid objects investigated his approach, so he placed the mask over his face and kept going.

Buildings seemed more weathered than he remembered, offering a sense of being hunkered down amidst a struggle. The Dome and its debris were gone, leaving a gaping skyline.

A change made starkly visible through absence. In this space he felt a low, heavy pulse—both attracting and repulsing. His intuition whispered, "foul splinter," and "soul-wound." *Later.* He made for a nondescript office building labelled, '6.'

The place looked much the same except for the removal of the six label. Fitting, as he'd outgrown the denomination. The plants in the entry room were withered and dead. Front desk empty, as usual. The door to the backroom opened to his touch. Stale alcohol and ignored clutter pervaded this former sanctum. There came a click of a firearm switching from tase to lethal.

"Take off the mask you grave robbing son of a bitch," said Rouey.

Mavrik turned, carefully removing the mask and letting it clatter to the floor. Rouey's finger twitched at the trigger.

"Can't be," he muttered.

"How long?"

Rouey blinked, seeing Mavrik but not fully comprehending.

"How long have I been away?"

"Away," said Rouey. "Not dead." His jaw tightened. "Three years. Each shittier than the last."

Mavrik nodded in resignation, feeling his friend's pain.

"You opened the box."

"Yes. Eldorado was revealed."

"And?"

*How to explain?*

Mavrik sat and Rouey joined him.

"You've lost your numanens," said Rouey. "Looks strange."

"Ikenna took them."

Rouey swore, then laughed sadly. "He owns everything! Kalubon is about to become his private enterprise. The whole planet able to be bought and sold to the highest bidder."

"The harvesting of Anima."

Realization dawned in Rouey's eyes. "Of course that's what it's for. The black pyramid goes operational tomorrow."

Ekundayo's grief washed through Mavrik, nearly carrying him away. "There's still time."

"He's got an army. Established to put down rebel factions. We can't fight him. I gave that up."

"What have you been doing?"

Mavrik noticed Rouey's eyes drift to an empty glass.

"I've been working with Nekane to heal soul-wounds. Oftentimes, all we can do is offer comfort."

Mavrik reached out, squeezing Rouey's shoulder, his eyes glistening. "That is enough. I'm proud of you, my friend. Your strength is my strength, your pain is my pain."

"It's been hard. I was so angry when they took you. Then sadness nearly claimed me when I accepted that you weren't coming back, that things were forever changed." He straightened, shaking off some of his fatigue. "And here we sit, same as always, like nothing happened."

"Through loss we've become more than we were. Nothing is set. We are alive. We may act."

"What did Eldorado show you that gives you this hope?"

"Connection." Mavrik stood, as if to leave. "Is there a hub where you and Nekane treat those with soul-wounds?"

"She converted her home, as well as a few neighbouring houses."

"Practically in the Harvester's shadow. Let's go."

As they walked, Rouey shared details about earthquakes, volcanic eruptions, tsunamis, temperature fluctuations, mass animal die-offs and looming food shortages. Witches were being silenced, essentially removed from public influence. Director Ikenna had enacted emergency policies to become High Facilitator, granting him exclusive decision-making powers. Meanwhile, soul-wounds continued to arise and each attempt to mitigate change seemed to further limit the options available to the common person.

The Harvester—Ikenna's newly fabricated pyramid—was being portrayed as a final solution, a means of escape from an increasingly dire situation, and many people were desperate enough to believe it.

A bright-eyed Aisha greeted them at the entrance, now fully in her teens. Her disbelief at Mavrik's appearance was plainly visible.

"Welcome," she said. "There are many that the Sleeper can offer choice to."

"He won't be joining us," said Mavrik. "Not like before."

"Oh…"

"May I still enter?"

"Of course," she said, blushing.

"Aisha has a knack for treating patients," said Rouey as they followed her inside. "Reminds me of Danya."

Walls had been removed to allow for open space, mostly occupied by narrow beds. Small partitioned rooms dotted the perimeter. People moved from bed to bed and room to room, tending to individuals of varying degrees of responsiveness.

"We're nearly maxed out," said Rouey. "Only a rare few heal enough to leave."

Aisha returned with Nekane; Mavrik was instantly aware of the woman's loving determination.

"This isn't the same witch who visited before," said Nekane.

Mavrik felt the pressure of her discernment, the depth of her insight.

"You are changed as well," he said.

He sensed golden dust floating throughout her presence, emanating to everyone in the vicinity.

"You are less, yet more," she said.

He realized what must be done, just as he knew that he needed to ask permission to collaborate with her radiance.

"Nekane, may I request your aid in seeking to empower the afflicted within this house?"

"You may." She smiled. "As long as no blades are involved."

"None. Only your hands."

Mavrik extended his with palms up and Nekane placed hers on top. Kallikrates flowed into existence, a part of him, like an instrument is to a master musician. The beautiful power poured out of him, merging with Nekane's goldenness. He focused on the invisible connections extending from the hub of her form. In his mind's eye, she became a river of light, spilling into dozens of streams.

Kallikrates weaved into the streams, strengthening their stability and supporting their direction. These reinforced light-streams each led to an individual with a soul-wound, as well as to Rouey, Aisha, and the other staff. Intensities of light were reflected amongst the different people: some only a sputtering candle and others, Aisha in particular, were like a miniature sun. Kallikrates amplified the connections, establishing a unified network.

Anima recognized the Selves as a whole in disparate aspects. Separation became less of an obstacle. Life knows movement, so Mavrik concentrated on freely offering opportunity for this process. Anima blazed across the network—life and death, joy and suffering.

Nature did as it always does and sought balance. Energy shifted between individuals, healing wounds and granting release. The beautiful power began to slow, Mavrik's influence within the network receding. The transfiguration was complete.

Many voices exclaimed, some long unused, all amazed at what had transpired, even if they didn't understand it.

"Thank you," Mavrik said to Nekane, squeezing her hands before letting go.

She wiped tears from her cheeks, delighted, as many of her patients returned from their stay at the crossroads. Some had moved on, and she sighed in relief, knowing they'd made a choice.

"You're not a serviteur anymore," she said.

"Only Leadership can sanction a witch."

"Leadership is supposed to represent the will of the people and we have not forgotten that, even if others have."

"What do you mean?"

Rouey stepped into their conversation. "There are those who follow Ikenna with blind loyalty, believing the Harvester is the only way forward. Leadership uses this support to implement changes while ignoring the opposition. Besides, it's getting easier to be labeled a rebel and then Law Enforcement kicks down your door."

Fear. An impulse Mavrik knew well. All sides mistrustful of the other, adamant that they were in the right. His heart pained for those caught in the struggle; hardening at the strings leading back to the puppeteer.

"It's time I spoke with the High Facilitator," said Mavrik.

"You'll be arrested," said Rouey.

"We can do so much good here," said Nekane.

"Both are just symptoms of a more foundational problem. I need to go to the source of the infection." He saw his friends exchange a worried look. "I won't be gone for three years this time."

* * *

The Harvester looked identical to the black pyramid that Mavrik had encountered in Ikenna's mind. It was so dark that it seemed to leech colour from the surroundings; an edifice whose hunger could never be satiated. Mavrik placed a hand on his chest in recognition of Ekundayo's suffering within this prison.

A slit of a door opened and a squad of armed guards approached with weapons drawn. Mavrik observed the wisps of vapour tumbling down the pyramid tiles, feeling the chill of sunlight being forcefully repulsed.

"Tell Ikenna that his cousin has come by for a visit."

There was a brief back and forth over radios before Mavrik was ushered inside. *Ekundayo, this is the first, and last, time that you/I are entering this door.*

Inside buzzed like a beehive as technicians ran tests, causing light arrays to flicker and machinery to hum. The guards led Mavrik to a spiral staircase upgraded to the crystal variety of Ekundayo's time. Down they went into an inverted version of the aboveground pyramid. Ikenna waited at the bottom—face strained, streaks of grey at his temples. He'd aged a dozen years in the past three. His analytical gaze scoured Mavrik for threats, for weaknesses, for opportunity and leverage.

A guard presented his firearm to the High Facilitator, who checked its setting, then nodded for the protection to leave.

"Hello, cousin, blood of my blood," said Mavrik.

Ikenna winced, scowling his way back into composure. "You survived."

"So have you." Mavrik glanced at the pedestal that he knew was to be used to create numanens containing Anima. "Opening the box linked this place to Errai. The pyramid draws power from the Shepherd King constellation."

"The system is fully automated and functional, except for one crucial aspect." Ikenna grinned, cold as the black tiles above. "A witch is required to act as a fulcrum, using kallikrates to join disparate forces. An archaic solution that I'm sure we will progress beyond in the near future."

"I doubt that."

Ikenna squinted, sensing that Mavrik knew more than he was telling. "I've got a viable candidate, but with your return it appears there is a new volunteer."

"Something you've dreamed of for some time?"

Ikenna shifted the firearm, unsettled by Mavrik's confident amusement.

"I know you seek to buy your way into the Alliance," said Mavrik. "That all of your claims of saving Kalubon are lies to fulfill your own ambitions."

"This world is a closed loop. I am progressing the system by granting access to all of the wasted potential."

Mavrik saw Ikenna's wound, as fresh as if only just received. And it was, because Ikenna had been holding onto it all of his life, constantly reopening this invisible injury while refusing to acknowledge its presence, denying healing for his Self and attempting to use power and control to placate this nagging, relentless emptiness.

"You think this will bring you an explanation," said Mavrik. "That the wealth and authority will justify any wrongdoings. That this achievement will finally bring balance to your silent suffering."

"You don't know anything about me. Your family has tried to take everything from mine. Even now."

"I accept you, even if I don't like you very much. We are connected in a network of belonging. We each have the ability to choose to manipulate or co-create. You are not alone. The weight of the world is not yours to carry."

"Enough lies. You want to steal what I have *earned*, corrupt what I *deserve*, just like Oberon betrayed my grandfather, but I will not be fooled." He motioned with the weapon. "Over to the pedestal. It's time."

Mavrik nodded, his hope for a change of heart from Ikenna extinguished. Words were not up to the task. A person believed what they saw and Ikenna couldn't see outside of the reality of his pain. Mavrik decided to show him another reality.

"All right," he said. "We'll see this through together."

Ikenna snapped orders into his radio, directing the technicians to begin the startup sequence. Mavrik picked up an orb from a stack behind the pedestal, feeling the cool solidity of this inert object. It dawned on him that this was how Ikenna viewed everyone and everything—individual objects fashioned for a specific purpose that could either give or receive energy. Mavrik sighed, acknowledging that until recently his perception of Anima hadn't been so different.

He carried the orb across the separating distance, holding it above the pedestal as his heartbeats alternated between fate and destiny.

"You know what to do," said Ikenna.

"Yes, but I've never done so. Knowing and living become harmonized through courage."

He set the orb into the cradle.

"You can put the weapon away," he said.

Ikenna's eyes bulged. "I could kill you, right now."

"You won't. You need me, have always needed me. Afterwards, I hope this relationship will evolve."

A light above the pedestal switched on, signalling the Harvester's readiness. Mavrik set his hands on the orb.

Lines of energy shot out from all directions, crackling intensely before settling into a regulated vibration. The lines coalesced inside of Mavrik, attuning his Being, activating kallikrates. The beautiful power rushed forth, transforming the lines into a dodecahedron. Mavrik sensed this geometric shape opening him up like a supremely sharp blade slicing through the lid of a container. The Harvester was finely crafted for the sole purpose of extracting Anima and it had found a golden hoard.

Mavrik shifted his awareness, focusing on the connections, securing the link between him and Ikenna. The Harvester escalated, almost eager to pillage and deposit. With kallikrates, Mavrik slowed the process, smoothening and broadening it beyond the targeted programming. Connection after connection linked together, more than the numanen had been designed to hold. Distantly, he heard Ikenna shout in alarm.

The connections autonomously arranged their pattern to mirror the Shepherd King constellation, with Mavrik in the place of Errai. He was the star, the star was him, and yet each remained uniquely constructed. The mirror images merged into an all-infusing light. Mavrik held tight to Ikenna as they were transported into another plane.

* * *

This wasn't Eldorado.

This was a place of heat and pressure, impermanence and eternity. Intimately familiar like a mother's embrace, yet as impersonal as the hand of death. Ikenna whimpered beside Mavrik. A blink and suddenly Anima was everywhere, in endless connections in all directions. Ikenna exclaimed, also aware of the bewilderingly overpowering environment. The connections all stemmed from a core source, a shifting sphere of light entwined with darkness.

An overpowering aliveness emanated from this core as it observed every molecule of Mavrik and Ikenna. The core's movements altered, establishing an unmistakeable realization of *presence*. Mavrik instinctively fell to his knees, head bowed. Ikenna trembled. The presence, now distinctly feminine, appraised the pair of interlopers.

"Kalubon," said Mavrik, "I beg forgiveness for our intrusion. I would have asked permission if I'd known how."

"YES," said this Being of creation-destruction. "I AM THE BLACK LOTUS."

Mavrik heard the self-remembering in Kalubon, the alignment of innumerable, far-reaching aspects.

"Children," said Kalubon, "you may look upon me."

Mavrik raised his head; the immensity of Kalubon shrinking to a merely gigantic form. A woman: dark and radiant, fierce, tameless, infinitely loving, as passionate as divine flame. Ikenna dropped, his entirety shaking. Mavrik's eyes were drawn to her swollen belly.

"A birth draws near," she said. "The offspring is yet to be determined. Evolution or extinction, these are humanity's twin paths. Each are in motion."

Her attributes became amplified at this proclamation; her strength crushing, her beauty terrible, her fierceness hostile, her love ecstasy. Ikenna screamed, cowering, unable to look away even as his body, mind and soul fractured. Mavrik moved to standing.

"I will do what I can to assist in this birth," he said.

Ikenna stuttered out, "...no..."

Kalubon's feminine form melded into an abstract combination of light and dark, expelling the men from her presence.

* * *

Sirens wailed inside the Harvester as technicians attempted to halt the overload. Mavrik stepped away from the pedestal, the orb now a bubbling puddle. Ikenna lay on the floor, catatonic. Maybe he would recover, maybe not. Mavrik hurried up the stairs, ready to share truth.

Those who were ready to hear would do so, and those not

yet ready would be shown compassion. Action was required; connections to be strengthened and co-created. Events might proceed peacefully, or they might not. Mavrik didn't know how things would play out, but he knew that change had arrived, a transition phase for the future of humanity.

The way of witches and the governance of Leadership were each ineffectual on their own; neither magic or technology alone could save them. They must evolve as individuals and as a society. The world had spoken.

Mavrik left the black pyramid behind, racing toward Nekane's, feeling alive in his body, mind and soul.

* * *

Humanity has so often relied on war as a method of decision-making, choosing the apparent straightforwardness of opponent versus opponent, us against them, and known contrasting unknown. Collective histories are thrown into conflict to dictate a desired future. The present is merely a means to an outcome. Differences are emphasized as a tool to reinforce duality: right and wrong, black and white, good and evil, but divisiveness only works when there is something to be divided—what do you do when the matter at stake is literally the world as a whole?

Who do you fight when the struggle is within yourself?

This precise dilemma confronted the people of Kalubon, arising one morning as if out of the blue, bearing a hidden weight that could only have been accumulated over much time. Society began splintering after the revelation of Mavrik's return from Pilgrimage, the lessons of Eldorado, and the warning given by the Black Lotus HerSelf.

Most people didn't want to fight, but they were frightened, and unresolved fear caused them to lash out. All seemed to sense that peace was unattainable in this transitory period as the rate of change continued gaining in velocity. Some saw enemies all around; feeling abandoned in their assumed separateness.

Some saw wounds in need of healing.

* * *

Mavrik travelled along golden streams of Anima, moving within unity as an individual, differences empowered by similarity. One did not take from the other, instead, one enhanced the other, supporting both. He flowed between connections until consciously returning to his physical form.

"An Alliance starship is nearing orbit," he said to Rouey.

"Then that cockroach Ikenna got a message through." Rouey shook his head. "For a person paralyzed from the neck down he is relentless."

"He believes that salvation resides in Alliance technology, his health in the stars, and only death and doom here on the ground."

"But you and he received the same message. How can the interpretations be opposites?"

"He chooses one path and I another."

"The starship will drop supplies to prop up their investment. He'll come after us again."

"Most likely."

Rouey frowned. "Your lack of concern is annoying."

Mavrik smiled, looking past Rouey to where Nekane led a group in training. "She is a marvellous teacher. See how she lovingly prepares these people to become healers? Aisha will soon be ready to teach as well." He nodded at Rouey. "And you, my friend, you have your own group to empower."

Rouey grumbled under his breath. "We're still outnumbered compared to those following Ikenna, those seeking to flee."

"For now. The balance is shifting though." Mavrik looked into the blue expanse, squinting at the brightness of the light. "Some may even succeed in getting off-planet. They will have to keep running, having gotten caught up in a larger version of what they fear."

Rouey sighed, momentarily overpowered by his concerns. "What if they're correct to flee a dying planet?"

Mavrik breathed calmly, evenly, peacefully—sensing the connections linking his Self to all those nearby and theirs to him.

"The world is not dying," he said. "Far from it."

Mavrik sensed the connections between humans intertwined with those of Nature, all joining to facilitate a creative, energetic process. All of the innumerable veins, neurons, cells and Beings of unified Kalubon. Within the coherence resided a lurking disruption, a deep wound inflicted by a million cuts.

"Humanity has caused injury," said Mavrik, "and if we are to take our place within the recalibration of the world then we must set to healing."

"Some would rather fight."

"As individuals and collectives we have taken much. As individuals and collectives we must now give."

Rouey smiled wistfully. "The simple sounds impossible."

"One and the same, my friend. One and the same."


The sweet chime of a hammer on steel rang out again and again.

A futuristic blend of grace and wisdom flowing through human hands.

A scent of sunlight warmed metal mingled with the sweat of service.

Mavrik hovered over his task, eyes focused and farseeing

as he brought the hammer down. Seven sets of hands from seven Selfs shaped the vertical form into a perfect ellipsoid. He contoured the rounded top and smoothed the sides of the mostly spherical object, creating the embodiment of a closed loop capable of embracing everything and therefore of expressing everything. This shape, egg-like and nearly as large as his own body was to function as a representation of the invisible, a symbol of truth. Anima transferred through his action, channeled from other planes and into the object, enlivening it so that it may become a nexus.

Such is the way of physical creation.

He was a serviteur, a person willing to navigate the space between known and unknown so that others might find their own way.

He retrieved his handpan, sitting and placing the drum on his lap. Mavrik played softly and tenderly, chanting in kallikrates while directing the expanding energy into the ellipsoid. The object was to be a reverse numanen, a sacred artifact capable of offering access to planes beyond the physical rather than containing the otherworldly. A living link between Kalubon and Eldorado for those who were willing to journey.

The beautiful power and his music thrummed into the standing ellipsoid, threading into every layer of its being. Mavrik's hands came to rest atop the drum as the vibration of his final chant completed the consecration.

The way was open for everyone who desired to change their fate in support of Kalubon's evolution.

# ACKNOWLEDGMENTS

My gratitude to those initial readers whose feedback was invaluable in rounding this story into form. Thank you: Karamvir, Cole, Amit, Simon and Will. My appreciation for Morgan Smith and the insight provided by her editing. A tip of the hat to Chance Clark for his timeliness and skill in creating a great cover. Lastly, thank you to those who choose courage. Stay true. Share love.

# ABOUT THE AUTHOR

Tyler Sehn lives in Alberta, Canada. He is a writer of poetry and fantasy. He's a basketball enthusiast (Go Raptors!), a hiker of moderate mountains and paddler of various rivers. A lover of the mysterious following questions where they may lead.

* * *

Contact: https://tylersehn.com/

* * *

Serialized fiction and author musings available at:
https://hawkandheronpublishing.substack.com/

# OTHER TITLES

**The Spiritbinder Saga** [Epic fantasy with a grimdark vibe]
Daughter of Shadow
Gods of Rua
Age of the Bloodless

**The Pale Queen** [A mythic adventure. A quick read.]